THE STRANGER NEXT DOOR

A Summer Hill Irregulars Mystery

Allie Ross

To my husband, Jim, my biggest fan and cheerleader, without whom this book would not exist. And to Roxie, who was the model for Maggie the boxer, and whom we lost in 2021. I will love you forever, little girl.

CHAPTER ONE

"Die! Die!" I screamed, pressing the trigger on my weapon and focusing on my helpless victims.

"Mom!" My son's whine penetrated my brain. "You sound like you're crazy. What are you doing? Everybody on the block can hear you! Maybe everybody in the neighborhood!"

I squinted at the young blonde Adonis who was staring at me, sunglasses perched on the top of his head, hands on his hips. His best friend, Max, stood slightly behind him, chewing on his bottom lip. His coffee-colored skin glistened with perspiration in the sunlight. I smiled at the boys, pushing my own glasses to the top of my head. "The squash bugs are destroying my zucchini," I explained reasonably. "I've tried everything else. This is war."

In spite of his best efforts one side of Nick's mouth ticked upward. My heart clutched. He looked so much like his father, my beloved Lars, who two years earlier had walked purposefully up to his secretary's desk, opened his mouth to speak, and dropped dead of a brain aneurism. Fortunately Lars, a successful attorney, had believed in life insurance and left us well provided for. We continued to live comfortably in our home, the mortgage paid off, and Nick's college fund remained intact. The money I earned through writing mystery novels paid our bills and provided a few extras from time to time. Next summer it would pay for Nick's college visits, including a trip all the way to California to see Nick's dream school, Cal Tech. It seemed impossible we'd reached this juncture. I wished I could slow down time. I'm sure many other parents wish the same. On the other hand, there were days when I couldn't wait to be an empty nester. Such were the ups and downs of parenting a teenager.

"Me and Max..." Nick began. I scowled at him. "Max and I" he corrected himself quickly, "are going to play some hoops. Can we take the car?" I stared at him. "May we take the car?" he asked, grinning now.

I smiled back. "Sure," I said. "Pick up some milk on your way home, OK?"

"Thanks, Mrs. O," Max said. "Man," he said in an aside to Nick "I thought *I* lived in the house of correction."

"Is Lexie going with you?" I asked, referring to his long-time friend who lived next door. Both boys stiffened. They were silent, exchanging undecipherable glances. "What's up?" I asked, eying them curiously.

My question was rewarded with the all too familiar teenaged shrug. I snatched the car keys from Nick's hand. "Spill." I commanded.

"It's no big deal, Mrs. O," Max said, shrugging again. "I guess we're not hanging around so much anymore – puberty and hormones and...and stuff."

I was speechless, which is not a normal condition for me.

As I tried to formulate a reply Lexie's mother walked down the driveway to her mailbox. Maybe I should say she sashayed. She was wearing a tiny bikini with a see-through sarong tied loosely around her hips. He long legs seemed to go on forever. The top of her bathing suit left little of her impressive bust line to the imagination. As she reached for her mailbox the sarong slipped to the ground, revealing a miniscule bikini bottom. "Oops!" She looked over. "Hi, boys." After a moment's pause, she smiled at me.

"Hi, Jackie." Liz showed off a perfectly flat stomach with taut abdominal muscles, the result of religiously following a challenging workout routine. I gave a silent sigh. I hadn't looked that good since college, and probably not even then. Strenuous exercise had never been my thing.

The boys stood staring open mouthed, eyes almost popping out of their heads. I frowned at her, then at the gaping adolescents. I cleared my throat. After a moment Liz seemed to receive my silent communication. "Oh," she said. She bent down to retrieve

the sarong and fastened it more securely around her.
"Darned thing doesn't want to stay tied."
"Hi, Liz," I said through gritted teeth. Max punched Nick lightly on the arm. He blinked and turned to leave. "Bye, Mom," he said, heading to the car.
"Come over for swim later boys," Liz called after them. Nick raised an arm in acknowledgement but kept on walking. Liz turned blue eyes on me. "Maybe you could come too," she said.
I'll see, Liz. I have a lot to do but thanks for the invitation."
"You've already picked enough zucchini to feed the whole street," she said. "Why don't we get together and do something fun?"
"I *am* having fun," I replied, picking up my gardening hose.
"Oh." She looked at me blankly. "Really?" She headed back toward her house, wobbling slightly on high heeled sandals.
My friend Marcia, who had been watching our interaction with interest from her front yard, crossed the street. "What was that about?" she asked.
I shook my head. "I don't know. Teenaged boys and the female form. I'd think she'd be a little more subtle."
Liz had always looked great. That hadn't changed, even now that she'd crossed into her forties. Even if she were dressed in a paper bag males of all ages would admire her. She couldn't help men's reactions to her. It was like attracting bees to honey. On the other hand, I expected her to act with some decorum around my son and his friends. On the other hand, maybe I was being overly stodgy. On the other hand – oh, phooey, there could only be so many hands.
"Nick and Max don't want to hang out with Lexie anymore. I wonder if it's because of Liz. Maybe she's too 'in your face' for them to handle."
Marcia scratched her nose, smearing garden dirt across her face. "Liz has been acting strangely ever since Dan left. She used to seem so normal." She thought a moment. "Well, relatively normal." She glanced toward her own house. "I'll see if I can get anything out of Bill." Marcia had twins Nick's age.

She switched her focus to the bottle in my hand. "Gave up on organic gardening again, huh?" She grinned.

I sighed. "It's almost Memorial Day. The bugs always start winning by the beginning of July but this year's they're really early."

"Memorial Day also means Liz's annual pool party. That could prove interesting now that Dan's not around."

"What does that mean?" I asked.

"Oh, you know...one hears rumors," Marcia replied.

"What kind of rumors?" I asked.

"For pity's sake, Jackie," Marcia said. "I can't understand how you're so out of the loop."

"I work for a living," I said a bit defensively. I thought about my current project, which was go ing more slowly than I would have liked.

"I know you do, Sweetie," Marcia said, touching my arm gently. "Even if you didn't, you probably wouldn't be interested in gossip anyway." She pulled a spent blossom from a plant. When she looked up, she was smiling mischievously. "But it can be so much fun. You wouldn't believe what you can hear at the gym or the grocery store. Or the hairdresser's." She reached out to touch my hair, which admittedly was overdue for a trim. I slapped her hand away. She laughed. "Especially at the hairdresser's."

"I get the hint," I said. "Believe it or not I actually have an appointment scheduled. But what rumors? Tell me."

"The rumor is that Liz has found herself a sugar daddy. Or maybe more than one..."

"Who?"

"That I haven't heard," Marcia said. "Stay tuned for breaking developments."

Marcia gave me a friendly wave and returned to her weeding.

I went back to my attack on the bugs, but my heart was no longer in it. I found myself fixating on Marcia's reference to Liz's separation. Maybe I wasn't being a good friend to Liz. We had never been close friends, but we had barbecues, went out to dinner from time to time, attended our children's games, concert and plays, and cheerfully gossiped about neighborhood goings-on for years. Then Dan moved out and things seemed to change. If I thought about it, they actually changed before then. Things between the two of them seemed stiff, a little forced. When they attended a social event is was almost as thought they had come separately, each one joining a different group and not paying much attention to the other. That was completely different from most of the years we had known each other. Dan had always seemed enthralled with his gorgeous wife and she had been proud of his professional achievements. I wondered what had changed.

Liz had been kind to me when Lars died. She took Nick to school events I couldn't attend and, along with her daughter Lexie kept Nick busy while I struggled with early widowhood. It wasn't the deep, unconditional love I received from Marcia, or Max's mother, Bernice, or my friend Linda at the end of the cul-de-sac. With them I could cry until I had no strength left, share my deepest fears and vent about the tedious and tortuous legal process involved with death. My relationship with Liz didn't have that sweetness, that depth, but it had been pleasant and welcome and important at the time.

I tried to be supportive of Liz when she and Dan separated, but she hadn't confided in me. I had no idea what had driven them apart, but I didn't need to know that to offer friendship. Once again, gestures of support had been appreciated but there was no real bonding. Nick had reciprocated Lexie's kind actions from the time of his dad's death, and mutual grief seemed to bring them together. I was sad that this appeared to be changing, and that they might be drifting apart. I wondered if the feeling was mutual or if only Nick was moving away.

I spotted a gray, triangular bug strolling along a zucchini leaf. "Die!" I reached out and squashed it in my fingers. It wasn't too icky, because I was wearing gloves. Anyway, this was war.

I moved to my tomato plants, testing the succulent fruit for ripeness. Starting the plants in a cold frame had led to a nice early crop. Visions of caprese salad danced in my head.

My thoughts returned to the scene at the mailbox. Maybe Liz

wasn't being provocative, I thought. After all, she *was* a spectacularly beautiful woman. Her luxurious auburn hair fell in soft waves to her shoulders. Her skin was milky white and flawless, her eyes a piercing blue. She toned her 5'10" body relentlessly and had abs any woman would covet. There was always a faint aura of sensuality around her, even at neighborhood parties, where she would concentrate deeply on what a man said to her, tilting her head slightly, and touching him gently when she talked.

I dropped a tomato into my basket and continued my self examination. Maybe – maybe Liz hadn't done anything inappropriate. I thought about her effect on the boys. Maybe, God forbid, I was jealous? I looked down at the dirty chino shorts I wore, at my ratty T-shirt, and my old lady gardening shoes. At forty-two I looked pretty good, trim from walking almost daily with my friends, riding my bicycle and working in the yard. I was attractive in an ordinary way, with straight blonde hair (already showing some gray), green eyes and a decent chin and nose, but I was no beauty. I certainly couldn't get away with wearing Liz's bikini. I thought a moment. Maybe I'd look into covering my gray hair, even add some highlights. Just the thought lifted my spirits. Vanity, thy name is Jackie.

I cleaned my garden tools, took a quick shower, put on a clean (and much more attractive) outfit, threw together a platter of cheese and crackers, and headed over to Liz's house. She had asked me to do something fun and I had rejected her. I hoped my peace offering would help.

Liz opened the door and stood uncertainly on her stoop. She had replaced the sarong with a floor length caftan which was less revealing but somehow still managed to showcase her curves.

"I'm sorry," I said, offering my plate. "I wasn't very nice this afternoon. You're right, we should do something fun. How about an adult beverage first?"

Liz smiled, taking the plate and ushering me inside. "Let's have a glass of wine," she said, leading me into her kitchen, "and then I need you to help me with something." We ate and chatted for a while before she picked up her glass and gestured for me to follow her. We walked into her bedroom. She disappeared into her walk-in closet briefly and came out carrying two dresses.

"I have a date," Liz said, "and I can't decide which dress to wear. What do you think?" She held up a deep green dress with a draped neckline. When she turned it around I saw that the back was non-existent until it hit the waistline.

"Pretty," I said noncommittally, taking a deep sip of my wine.

"And then there's this one," Liz said, holding up a short sheath with a plunging neckline.

"Where are you going?" I asked. Frankly I couldn't imagine wearing either dress, especially in Summer Hill, Virginia, but then again, I didn't have Liz's height or toned body. Even if I did, I'd opt for something that left a little more to the imagination. OK, let's be honest. It would leave a *lot* more to the imagination.

"Dinner in town," she replied. "And then, who knows?" She raised her eyebrows suggestively and smirked.

In the driveway a car door slammed. I heard rapid footsteps and Lexie appeared in the doorway. "Mrs. O!" She hurried to me, smiling, and gave me a brief hug.

Lexie pivoted quickly to her mother, eyeing the dresses she'd laid out on the bed. "Are you going out again tonight?" she asked, her voice glacial.

Liz mirrored her daughter's body language. "And what if I am?"

Lexie did the teenaged shrug thing. "Whatever."

"Nick will be home tonight," I interjected. "Would you like to come for dinner?"

Lexie smiled briefly. "No, thanks, Mrs. O. I have to work. I'll see you both later." The glance she threw at her mother was still cold. She trotted down the hall toward her bedroom.

"Teenagers," Liz said with a weak smile.

"They're a challenge," I agreed. "Never a dull moment."

"You're not kidding," Liz replied "I just wish Lexie would try to understand..." Her voice trailed off.

"I'd better let you get ready," I said, standing and putting my wineglass on the nightstand. "We'll get together another time."

Liz nodded absently, focused on her sartorial choices.
I peeked into Lexie's room as I walked to the front door. She was standing in front of a mirror, listlessly brushing her hair.
"Lexie?" I said tentatively.
She smiled tremulously at me through the mirror. "It's all right, Mrs. O. Just mother and daughter stuff. Say 'hi' to Nick for me, OK?"
"Sure," I said. But as I left the house I turned around to stare at it. I couldn't help but wonder what was going on and I also couldn't help but worry about Lexie and her mother.

CHAPTER TWO

The next day I sat down to start a new project my agent had encouraged me to take on, temporarily putting my other one aside. I was starting to feel it needed some major changes and wasn't quite ready to tackle them. As to the new book, 'coerced into taking' might be a more accurate phrase than 'encouraged'.

Six weeks ago my agent said to me, "Your publisher wants you to write a culinary series."

I blinked. "That's been done," I said. "Many times."

"Yes," she said, "but they don't have an entry in the field. They want one. They think they need one."

"Why me?" I protested. "I know nothing about the food industry."

My agent smiled. She looked like a barracuda or, even worse, a shark. "They have faith in you."

I remained silent.

"You're a good researcher," she said. "It won't take you long to understand the business."

"I have to deliver another book in the series I'm already working on," I whined.

"It wouldn't be the first time you wrote two books in a year," she pointed out.

I said nothing.

"The advance would pay for the car you're going to buy Nick," she said.

"Nick is saving for a down payment," I replied. It was her turn to remain mute.

I thought about all the times I found myself stranded while Nick drove to friends' houses, to sporting events, to school, on dates... Was I going to buy Nick a car? Of course, I was.

"No recipes," I said.

My agent raised one eyebrow. "But including recipes and crafts is so popular. It really sells."

"I can't imagine why anyone would cook out of the back of a mystery novel," I said, neglecting to mention the hours of fun I'd had trying recipes from Julie Hzyz's White House chef series and Katherine Hall Page's catering series. And then there was Joanne Fluke and Cleo Coyle and...OK. Point taken.

The silence dragged on. I leaned back and crossed my arms across my chest. "No recipes," I repeated, but a little less resolutely. I do make an incredible lasagna, if I say so myself. Of course, it comes out a little different every time, so coming up with a recipe could be a challenge. Oh, never mind. No recipes. Period.

My agent smiled, "I suppose if we need recipes we can hire someone for that."

And so I researched. I read every reputable book I could find about becoming a chef, owning a restaurant or catering. I watched cooking shows on TV and occasionally cooked along. I even bought a book on how to publish a cookbook, on the off chance that I changed my mind about developing recipes.

I was lucky enough to be able to shadow instructors at the local cooking school and audit some classes. I braised, I sautéed, I broiled, I roasted. I made and ate lots of wonderful food and felt my waistband tighten.

The lectures on hygiene freaked me out. I spent an entire weekend washing every dish, pan and utensil in my kitchen. I sanitized every surface. I threw out my old cutting board and bought a new one just for chicken. That made sense. Then I bought another just for fish and one for everything else. I don't know why I did that.

I also threw out all my plastic leftover containers. I don't know why I did that either, except that it allowed me to buy some pretty pastel ones with snap on lids.

I banished the dog's bowl to the laundry room and the cat's to the sun porch. I alphabetized my spices (true confession – I do that twice a year anyway). I bleached the inside of the refrigerator. Then I threw out anything that smelled or tasted like bleach, which was basically the entire contents.

I was about to attack the grout on the tile floor with a wire brush when Nick put his arm around me. "I'm moving in with Max," he announced. "His mother said I could." I tried to gauge his seriousness. "*And* I'm calling Grandma. I'm telling her you've gone off your rocker and you need medication. She'll be on the next plane down."

I thought a moment. I loved my mother, but...That evening dirty dishes sat in the sink while we ate popcorn and laughed ourselves silly at an old Mel Brooks movie. The old normal felt good. Nick didn't move. My mother didn't fly in. All was right with the world. Except for starting the new book.

And now I sat in my home office, surrounded by research materials, starting work on a new series. I'd decided that my protagonist would be a food critic. I was carefully outlining her biography, trying to identify the things that would make her pop off the page. I was starting to like her when I heard a tap on the French doors across from my desk.

Lexie smiled at me through the glass, waving a brightly colored envelope. I beckoned her inside.

"Mom wanted me to bring you the invitation to the pool party," she said, passing me the envelope. "And she says to please bring your potato salad. It's really, really awesome, so I'm asking you to bring it too. Pretty please?" She grinned.

Hmm...maybe I should rethink recipes. "Be happy to," I said. "Do you have a few minutes? Maybe we could have a soda and catch up."

Lexie agreed and soon we were sitting in the sunroom, sipping diet sodas with lime. I studied Lexie as she prattled on about her summer job at a local clothing store. She was a pretty girl. She wasn't drop dead gorgeous like her mother, but in come ways I preferred her looks. She seemed more approachable somehow.

Her hair was more of a carrot color, naturally curly and framing her face, cut chin length. Her nose was upturned like her father's and sprinkled with freckles which she naturally hated. I thought she was adorable.

When she was little Lexie had borne a strong resemblance to Little Orphan Annie. For a while Liz turned into a stage mother, trying to capitalize on her daughter's cuteness. Unfortunately for Liz, Lexie didn't cooperate. She couldn't sing, hated to dance, and wiggled her way through a modeling audition. Finally, Liz threw in the towel, much to Dan's relief. Lexie was allowed to take the swimming lessons she wanted and joined the swim team, where she excelled. She played a mean game of tennis also, and she and Nick spent many happy hours hitting balls in our back yard or competing on the neighborhood tennis courts.

Sometimes I wished she and Nick would date, but that would just complicate their friendship. Wisely, I chose to let them decide if they wanted more. After all, they were just sixteen. It was too soon for a serious romantic relationship. At least it had been in my day. Kids grow up so quickly anymore.

I was actually glad Nick didn't have a serious girlfriend yet. Watching the way other kids his age fell all over each other gave me a serious case of heartburn. I considered slipping him some condoms just in case but nixed that idea. We had 'the talk'. Man, was that awkward. Turned out he probably knew more than I did. Oh, yuck! So I kept my fingers crossed and my eyes open. So far so good. I think.

Lexie had stopped talking and sat picking at the label on her soda bottle.

"Lexie," I started.

"I miss my dad," she blurted. Her eyes were moist with tears when she looked up.

I was surprised. Dan had always been actively involved with Lexie, at least when he wasn't traveling. "How often do you get to see him?" I asked.

I got the teenage shrug again. "It's supposed to be every other weekend, but he's traveling more than ever. And then when he tries to change dates, Mom makes it really hard for him." Tears ran down her cheeks. "Last night he called and they had a terrible fight. Mom hung up on him and she wouldn't let me call him back." Now she was crying in earnest. I shifted to sit next to her and hugged her shoulders. "Have you tried to talk with your mother?" I asked.

"She won't listen." Lexie grabbed a napkin off the table and dabbed at her eyes. "When Dad's out of town she's always going out and coming back late and leaving me alone. But when Dad's in town she comes up with things to do so I can't see him or she's busy setting me up on blind dates."

"Blind dates? I though you were going out with Rob," I said, referring to a boy in her class.

"We broke up." The sobs started again. "He's going out with Suzie. She's a cheerleader and she's really pretty. I'm not."

Oh dear.

"You certainly are," I replied stoutly. "Rob's a jerk." I couldn't picture him, but I was sure I didn't like him. "So who are these blind dates of yours?"

"Guys from the college," Lexie tossed her soggy napkin into the trash. "Dad doesn't like it. He says they're too old for me."

I certainly agreed with him. "What do you think?" I asked carefully.

"Most of them are OK," said, "but I'd just as soon hang out with my friends most of the time." She hesitated. "And sometimes they want to do more than kiss and...and I don't want to."

"Lexie!" I exclaimed. "Have any of them forced you to do something you didn't want to?"

She shook her head. "No. But I feel bad when I say no."

I turned her to face me. "Don't ever, ever feel bad about that. You're doing the right thing. And if you want, I can show you a couple defensive moves just in case." I had taken self-defense classes after Lars died. She looked surprised. "That might be cool."

I tried to relax and took a deep breath. "Have you talked to your mother about this?"

She nodded miserably. “She says I’m right, too, but then she sets me up on another date.” She kicked her chair. “It’s like she can’t go without a man and she thinks I can’t either. It’s her fault Dad left. She pushed him away, always wanting to go out even when he just got home and was tired. We couldn’t just hang around the house and watch movies like a normal family. That wasn’t good enough for Liz! And now all she wants to do is shop and go out with guys I don’t even know.”

She balled up her fists “I hate her! I’d be better off if she were dead!” She saw my stricken face and clapped her hands over her mouth. “I’m sorry, Mrs. O! I didn’t mean it! How could I say something so awful? I’m sorry!” Lexie sprang to her feet and bolted from the room.

Maybe I should have followed her, but I didn’t.

CHAPTER THREE

After Lexie left, I tried to go back to work, but I couldn't concentrate. I picked up my pen and stared at my writing pad. Nothing. I stood up and did some calisthenics, jumping jacks and toe touches. Still nothing. I fed the cat, put in a load of wash and cleaned the kitchen counters. If Nick hadn't taken Maggie to the park, I would have done that too. Nothing, nothing, nothing except nagging worries about Lexie. I slapped on my gardening hat and stepped outside to water the tomatoes. I stood absentmindedly spraying water until I spotted Bernice walking her dog down the street. For a moment I hesitated, but made a quick decision. I needed desperately to talk to someone about Lexie and Liz. Lexie hadn't sworn me to silence and I wasn't sure I would have agreed if she had tried. Bernice would be perfect to talk to. She wouldn't gossip – at least not about something like this. And she would never divulge a confidence.

"Hey! Bernice!" I waved my arms and trotted to the end of the driveway. Bernice smiled and her dog sat beautifully beside her. Maggie would have had me trussed with the leash like a chicken. But she was a puppy and we were working on it, along with a myriad of other things.

"What's up?" When Bernice smiled the entire area around her lit up. Her teeth were the most dazzling white I'd ever seen. She was willow slim with a swanlike neck and a straight, patrician nose. Her black tousled corkscrew curls framed her face perfectly, accentuating high cheekbones set in a face the color of milk chocolate. In other words, she was stunning. How I ended up on this street of gorgeous women I'd never know.

Anyone who was taken in by Bernice's good looks alone, however, was in for a surprise. Sure, she had had a successful modeling career for many years. She gave that up after her husband, Ray, swept her off her feet and they started having children. Bernice, in between wiping noses, diapering babies, and appearing on Ray's arm at charity events while he pursued his football career, found time to return to college and earn her PhD in mathematics. She was now a tenured professor at a nearby university. Ray, who retired from sports at a ridiculously young age, also turned to academia and now served as principal of Summer Hill's high school. They had three handsome, gifted children with perfectly straight teeth. Natural. No orthodontics needed for that family. Of course. Max, Nick's buddy, was the oldest of their brood. Like his father, Max was a stellar athlete. He favored both parents academically and had his heart set on becoming a doctor.

It should have been easy to hate a woman like Bernice and be envious of her and her perfect family. However, she was kind and sensitive and had a wonderfully dry sense of humor. If she was your friend she was loyal and steadfast and always had your back. Bernice was my friend. It meant the world to me.

Now she scrutinized my face carefully. "What's up, girlfriend?"

"Let's sit," I said, gesturing to the comfy chairs on my front porch. I filled Bernice in on my conversation with Lexie.

"Teenagers tend to exaggerate," Bernice said. "And adolescent girls almost always go through a phase where they hate their mothers." She smiled knowingly.

"So you think I'm overreacting," I replied, feeling some of the tension leave my body.

"Not necessarily," Bernice replied. My tension swept back in and magnified. Bernice tucked one leg under her, her favorite position for a good gossip. "I've been hearing some rumors about Liz lately, especially at the gym. She's been working out a lot more recently, and one of the ladies in my aerobics class told me Liz was going out with one of the personal trainers."

"Oh, come on," I protested. "They're all half her age!"

Bernice grinned. "Be that as it may, tongues are wagging." She held a hand out in front of her, hands curved like claws. "Maybe she's turning into a cougar. Meow!"

I laughed. "Highly unlikely."

"Is it?" Bernice leaned forward, more serious now. "Marcia told me about Liz's performance at the mailbox yesterday. You know, teenaged boys can be pretty stupid, particularly when it comes to S-E-X."

"Why are you spelling?" I asked, looking to see if her eight-year-old had wandered into the yard. She just laughed.

"Max and Nick told me they're not hanging out over there anymore," I offered.

"May be just as well. No forty something is going to teach my baby about the birds and bees," Bernice declared.

"Are you taking this cougar thing seriously?" I asked.

"Probably not," she admitted, straightening her legs. "Ray and I saw Liz having dinner with someone at La Rive last weekend. Nice looking man, grey hair, distinguished." She chewed her lip. So that was where Max got the habit! "I felt like I should have known the man but I couldn't place him," she said.

"Did Ray recognize him?" I asked.

Bernice laughed. "You know Ray! He's the height of respectability. I'd have to pry it out of him if he did. I could try though if you think it's important. This guy and Liz seemed pretty friendly, sharing food off their plates and laughing a lot."

"That didn't take long," I said. "Dan hasn't been gone more than a few months."

"And the divorce isn't close to being final," Bernice said. "I hear they're fighting about..." she rubbed her fingers together "money."

"Where in the world do you hear these things?" I asked.

Bernice laughed. "Girl, you need to get out more."

I thought about my book deadlines. "Like that's going to happen." I stretched "I'm still worried about Lexie."

"Ray can hook her up with her school counselor. Do you want me to make sure he does?"

I thought a moment. "No, let's wait. She's a sharp young lady and she'd figure out I was behind it. I don't want her to stop confiding in me."

Bernice nodded. "Makes sense. I'll keep my ears open and if I hear anything that sounds important, I'll let you know."

"Well, it's been fun," I said, rising, "but I need to get back to work."

Nick rounded the corner onto our cul-de-sac with Maggie at his side. Wonder of wonders, she was heeling. She started to pull when she saw Bernice and me. Bernice's bichon popped to its feet, tail wagging madly. The dogs sniffed each other and then Maggie made a play bow. The bichon turned in circles, barking excitedly. Both dogs were set free and ran into my back yard, jumping and growling playfully.

"How was the park?" I asked my son.

"Good," he replied in the terse manner reserved for teenaged boys. He hesitated. "I saw something kind of weird though."

"What was that?" I asked in what I hoped was an encouraging manner.

"I saw Lexie's mom with some guy. He looked kind of young and really buff."

Bernice and I exchanged glances.

"Here's the weird part." Nick rushed his words, a sign he was agitated. "I saw her dad, too, watching them. He was hiding behind a tree, like in some lame spy movie. He had a camera and a really mad expression on his face. I turned away for a second to throw the ball for Maggie and when I looked again he had vanished." He snapped his finger. "Poof! Gone just like that. Weird, huh?"

Weird indeed.

"What was Mrs. Williams doing with the man you saw?" Bernice asked, trying to appear casual.

"They were just talking. Then he gave her a piece of paper or something and they both left."

Nick whistled for Maggie. Bernice clipped the bichon to her lead. She raised one eyebrow at me. I grimaced back.

"Oh," Nick said before entering the house. "Mrs. Williams has a new car. A red BMW. Really sweet. Mr. Williams took a picture of that too." He shook his head. "Man, he looked even madder when he saw that car." He perked up. "I wonder if she'll let Lexie drive it. That would be too cool." He vanished into the house, leaving

Bernice and I eying each other speculatively. So Dan and Liz had been arguing, he was taking pictures of her with another man, she had a pricey new toy and they were fighting over money. This was going to get really messy, if it wasn't already.

CHAPTER FOUR

By the time Memorial Day rolled around I was feeling pretty pleased with myself. I had finished the first draft of my non-culinary mystery and put it away for a few days. I liked to let a book bubble in the back of my brain for a period of time before I began editing. During that period some of my best ideas sometimes struggled their way out of my subconscious mind.

I was well into the outline for the new book. In addition, I had found time to can some pickles and freeze a batch of pesto. The war against the squash bugs continued unabated but for the time being at least I seemed to have the upper hand. Neighbors were starting to avert their eyes when I came by with vegetable offerings. Soon they'd be running away and locking their doors.

Lexie hadn't visited. I had seen her coming and going but she always seemed to be in a hurry. Nick remained mum about the situation next door. I supposed I had to give him credit for loyalty to his friend.

Memorial Day promised to be a scorcher, a harbinger of things to come in southeast Virginia, so I made the potato salad early in the morning. Even so the steam from boiling potatoes and frying bacon made the kitchen damp and hot. I chopped onions, pickles, celery and olives, tossed together my special sauce and stuck the concoction in the refrigerator. I was happy to escape to my wraparound porch and nurse a glass of lemonade.

The house looked festive. I had tied red, white and blue bunting on the porch railings and an American flag fluttered in the breeze. In honor of the occasion I had also tied a red, white and blue bow onto Maggie's collar. A hiss and a swipe with unsheathed claws convinced me not to try the same thing with the cat. Now she lay sulking under Nick's bed and Maggie snored softly in the shade under my feet.

Some of the younger children in the neighborhood were staging a makeshift parade. One young girl jogged by pushing her baby brother in a stroller bedecked with patriotic ribbon. The baby was wearing an Uncle Sam hat and seemed to be waving his rattle in time to music played by members of our fife and drum core. A large dog resembling a small horse pulled a red wagon. Children and some of their line skating parents glided by, waving and laughing. I waved back and smiled. Our town loved the holidays. The day would end with a fireworks display in our local park.

As I watched, Lexie jogged down her driveway and grabbed the newspaper. We hadn't talked since her outburst and based on her absence from our house I suspected she was avoiding me, but her wave seemed friendly. As I said, Nick refused to comment. He did tell me, however, that she had spent a weekend with her father and seemed happier than before she did so. Bernice had no new gossip to share. Marcia's son Bill refused to talk about Lexie, but Marcia wasn't sure he knew anything that would have shed light on things in any event.

There had been no new sightings of Dan Williams. Liz dashed about the neighborhood in her red BMW convertible, inciting envy in many hearts, not all of them male. The car inspired me to spend time on the internet, starting to investigate a car purchase for Nick. I was beginning to think I'd give him my current vehicle and pick up something newer for myself. Whatever it was wouldn't be able to compete with Liz's flashy new wheels, but that was fine with me.

At my feet Maggie raised her head and chuffed softly. I glanced across the street and saw Marcia exit her house carrying a big bowl of something. Today her dark hair was cut short in a spiky style, artfully sticking out around her scalp. One never knew what to expect from Marcia, who changed hairstyles as frequently as some women changed shoes. At least her hair wasn't purple today. She was tiny, barely over five feet tall, with a tight, limber physique reflecting her history as a college gymnast. She still coached the local girls' team and could still do a mean back flip.

Personally, turning upside down made me nauseous. Several months ago Marcia had talked me into trying aerial yoga with her. It was interesting, doing yoga positions in the air, sometimes upside down, sometimes sideways. Near the end of the session the instructor gave me a shove while I was hanging head down. I squealed and I think I uttered some words no one, including me, realized I knew. At least that's what Marcia and the teacher told me. I distinctly remember throwing up on the instructor's foot. Needless to say, I haven't been invited back.

Marcia had a gamine look, with dark eyes and a heart shaped face, resembling Audrey Hepburn dining at Tiffany's or Leslie Caron spinning through Paris. At least, she resembled them when her hair wasn't striped or some outlandish color. Then all bets were off.

As I mentioned earlier, she was our resident free spirit and artist. She was forever hanging new and interesting decorations on their door and placing sometimes unidentifiable objects in their front flowerbeds. The rest of us had finally persuaded her that more was not better, and we were no longer confronted by fields of ceramic mushrooms or drowned out by the clinking of rows of wind chimes.

Currently Marcia's front flowerbed was host to a group of whimsical fairies. Their dresses were made of canning jars, their wings of kite material. Curly moss served as hair and was glued to wooden balls on which were painted large eyes, button like noses and smiling lips. Marcia had decorated the jars with strings of beads, making it look as though the fairies were wearing 1920's flapper dresses.

Normally I am firmly in the "less is more" camp, preferring to let my plants speak for themselves. I had to admit, however, that the fairies were adorable. Moreover, I wanted one. I really, really wanted one.

Marcia stepped off her porch and saw me eying her collection. "Take one," she said. She didn't have to offer twice. I dithered a few moments before choosing a fairy with lime green and hot pink wings. I scurried back up my driveway, grinning from ear to ear, clutching my treasure to my chest.

In spite of reminding me of a wood sprite herself, Marcia was a surprisingly down to earth parent. She was open and accepting to a large degree and it wasn't unusual for a neighborhood teenager to confide in her before his or her own parent. She often surprised them. Marcia had a strong sense of right and wrong and was able to set clear limits with her children. More than once she had set someone else's child on a better path. Those children left her confessor's box perplexed, wondering how someone who seemed so quixotic could actually be so much like their own mother or father.

Marcia's exuberant personality was balanced out by her accountant husband, Bob. He grinned and threw me a casual wave as they headed toward the street. They were trailed by their twins, Bill and Kevin, who were too busy pushing each other and throwing fake punches to see me.

Time to head to Liz's barbecue. I sniffed the air appreciatively. It smelled like Liz was cooking her famous ribs.

"Sorry, Maggie," I said to my pup, who was anxiously eying me. "You're not invited." I threw some toys into her crate, made sure she had fresh water and a snack, grabbed the potato salad and headed next door.

"Yoo hoo!" Linda from the end of the street trotted up beside me. "Potato salad?" I nodded. "I did something different for a change," she said. She held up a six pack. "German beer instead of U.S." I shook my head." You are hopeless." Linda ranked cooking right down at the level of cleaning toilets and kept our gourmet market in business singlehandedly. A busy hospital administrator, she sported a gray bob with every hair firmly in place and a figure that, while trim, had curves in all the right places.

"No date this year?" I teased. She was notorious for showing up to every neighborhood party with a new man in tow. Someone had yet to make a second appearance.

She shook her head cheerfully. "I'm in a hiatus period," she replied. "Just me and the cat and we're perfectly happy to keep it that way for a while. You know the old saying about women and men and fish without bicycles." Linda had never married, except that she was married to her job, she liked to say. She lived in an immaculately kept house with her Persian, Miss Kitty, whom she often walked on a leash. At least once a year Linda and Miss Kitty would haul out their RV and head out on a road trip.

Linda liked to brag that she had the world's best-looking cat and enjoyed showing off pictures of Miss Kitty on the road, usually sharing the picture with an attractive man they had met along the way. Apparently, Miss Kitty was as attractive to men as is a new puppy. She was a contented cat and seemed to take all the traveling and men in stride.

"Where's Miss Kitty?" I asked.

"She hates fireworks," Linda replied. "And there are bound to be some tonight, don't you think?"

"Do you know something I don't?"

She grinned mischievously. "Rumors are flying. I heard Dan might put in an appearance at the party."

I shuddered. "Rumors seem to be doing that flying thing around here a lot lately. Here, you take the potato salad. I've changed my mind about going." I pretended to turn around.

Linda cuffed me on the shoulder. "Just kidding about the party. Miss Kitty took some cat valium though. Loud noises really do freak her out."

"Do you honestly think Dan might show?" I asked, shifting the salad to my other arm.

"No, I don't think he'd do that to Lexie," Linda replied. "Although I hear he's showing up in some unexpected places." She raised her eyebrows. "I also heard he's having Liz tailed."

I groaned. "First Bernice, now you. Where do you hear these things?"

"You need to get out more."

Déjà vu all over again.

The party was in full swing when we arrived. A group of neighborhood teens, including Nick, Lexie and Max were playing a spirited game of water volleyball in the pool.

Surreptitiously I looked around for a fit personal trainer but saw none. No sign of an older gentleman with white hair either. I did see several college age boys talking with some of the local kids. Lexie's friend Anna, who was going to be a senior in the fall, flirted outrageously with a tall blonde. The boys were all good looking, obviously athletes with muscular arms and legs and carved abs. It all looked perfectly innocent, but most of the girls were much younger than Anna. I noticed more than one gimlet eyed mother keeping tabs on the situation.

In a far corner Liz was engaged in animated conversation with a man I didn't recognize. From time to time she'd throw her head back and laugh, touching his arm or shoulder.

"If she touches my husband like that, I'll knock her block off," muttered Alice, who lived around the corner.

I turned to look at her in surprise. "Sorry," she said, pulling a funny face. "It's just that Liz considers herself a free agent these days and she's interested in playing ball in a lot of places."

"Really?" I said noncommittally. Where did people get hold of these rumors?

Alice laughed. "It's all gossip," she admitted. "I like Liz, really I do. And a lot of people are jealous of her. I mean, she's drop dead gorgeous, she has this great house, fabulous clothes, a perfect daughter..."

"And a husband who left her," I pointed out.

Alice sighed. "True. She could be putting on a show, I suppose." She glanced at Liz, who had shifted her attention to someone else. "But men can be so gullible." A little girl ran up to her and tugged at her mother's shorts. "I think I'm wanted," Alice laughed as she let her daughter pull her toward a table groaning with food.

I spotted Bernice's husband poking at something on the grill. Ray considered himself the African-American version of barbecue celebrity chef Bobby Flay and there was no telling what he was concocting.

I grabbed a glass of wine and sidled up to him. "What are you cooking?" I asked.

"Grilled avocado," he responded. "Hand me that platter. They have to come off fast." I complied. I wrinkled my nose at the fruits, which didn't look particularly appealing. "That's it?" I asked. Ray threw a large handful of shrimp onto the grill. "No. I'm going to make a spicy shrimp salad and put it into the avocados." That sounded good. Hmmm... maybe it could go at the end of my novel. No, stop thinking that way. I had put my foot down. No recipes! But still...

"Bernice told me about Lexie and her mother," Ray said out of the side of his mouth.

"What's your take?" I asked, grateful he had raised the subject.

Ray expertly flipped the shrimp. "I was watching them earlier. Hand me that bowl, would you?" He scooped up the shrimp. "I'm not a psychologist but I know what to look for. Nothing I'm seeing strikes me as particularly unusual." He dumped the shrimp onto a wooden board and started chopping. "Teenagers tend to take divorce hard though, and they often think they're to blame. They're prone to being self-centered, some might even say narcissistic, in any event and can't really see the big picture. Everything's about them. Lexie will probably get through this just fine. Some counseling couldn't hurt. Just in case."

"In case what?" I asked.

"In case Lexie is feeling worse about herself than shows." Horrible thoughts of suicide, drug abuse and self-mutilation crossed my mind. How could I not have kept more of an eye on Lexie, tried to talk to her again?

"I was thinking of asking Ed Scruggs to talk to her." He gestured with his knife toward a tall, lean man with graying sideburns and a neat short beard who was sipping a beer and joking with Marcia's husband. Ed was an Episcopal priest who lived two streets over with his wife and four daughters. "The kids all know him from coaching local sports. He's a great guy, and I think he's a very talented therapist." Ed had come later in life to the priesthood, after obtaining his master's degree in psychology and working as a therapist in private practice for several years.

"Sounds like a great idea," I replied.

"What I don't understand is why Liz is giving Dan such a hard time about seeing Lexie. Judges have little patience with custody disputes where teenagers are involved." Ray by now was tossing shrimp and other ingredients together in the bowl. "She must be trying to get leverage over something else."

"Like money," I said.

"Money," Ray agreed. "I can't see how she can afford that BMW unless Dan's already settled some money on her and I know for a fact that he hasn't."

"Do tell," I said, handing him a beer.

"Shoot, I didn't mean to say that," Ray said. "I had a couple drinks with Dan last week," Ray continued. "He's not giving her anything he doesn't have to. In fact, if he were a violent man I'd worry about what he might do. He's that angry. He claims Liz has gone completely off the rails and is doing everything she can to turn Lexie against him. He and I have been good friends for a very long time by now, and I'm not going to let a divorce destroy that. It happens all too often but it's not happening to my friendships." I saluted him for his sentiment. He made a shooing gesture. "Now go away and let me finish my masterpiece."

I started to leave but turned around again. "You don't really think Dan would hurt Liz, do you?"

"Not the Dan I know. But if anything happened to her and I was a cop he'd be my prime suspect, knowing how upset he is these days. Now go away."

The rest of the party passed uneventfully, thank goodness. I saw Anna pass her phone number to the blonde boy. Lexie spent some time talking to a college boy with a crooked smile and sparkling blue eyes. From what I could tell she seemed to be enjoying the attention. I suppressed a smile when I saw Nick cast an irritated glance in her direction.

"Time to get going if we're going to get a decent spot for the fireworks," Marcia announced as dusk approached. The adults scurried around cleaning up and gathering children.

"You go ahead," Liz said to me, taking a pile of used paper plates from my hands. "I think I'm going to pass this year. I should be able to see the highest ones from here." She turned a deaf ear to my offers of help and soon I found myself walking up the driveway.

I let Maggie out of her crate and encouraged her to relieve herself in the back yard. We played a spirited game of keep away (boxers don't like to return things you throw) for a few minutes. The pop! pop! pop! of family fireworks sounded around us. Maggie ran to me and pressed against my leg, shaking. Oh, dear. My precious pup was terrified of the noise. She'd never heard fireworks before. I decided to sit in my sunroom and watch what I could of the community display. If even that noise frightened Maggie we'd move into the main part of the house where it wouldn't be so loud. After all, I'd seen plenty of fireworks in my day. Maggie and I settled down on the couch and I stroked her silky fur gently. Soon her eyes closed and she seemed relaxed, although loud noises made her twitch.

I must have dozed off, because I was awakened by the sounds of slamming car doors and teenaged voices. Pop! Another firecracker. There was a brief pause, and then the sound of what sounded like one rocket wailing after another. Maggie sat up straight, threw her head back and howled. The rockets shrieked and Maggie howled in reply. I'd never heard so many rockets fired in a row. It was strange. I opened the door to the outside. That's when I realized that the noise wasn't rockets. It was screaming.

CHAPTER FIVE

Lexie stood in her driveway shrieking. Her hands were clutching at her hair, tears were streaming down her face and she was alternately jumping up and down and bending forward at her waist as though trying to catch her breath. Nick and Max raced toward her from our driveway. Bob and Marcia practically flew out of their front door. "I called 911!" Marcia shouted. The street was flooded with light as neighbors threw open doors and ran toward Lexie. I saw Bernice silhouetted in her doorway, holding her younger children back.

"My mom! My mom! My mom!" Lexie screeched. "She's dead! My mom's dead!" Nick threw his arms around her. Max and their friend Bill did the same to form protective circle.

Bob and I glanced at each other and in silent agreement charged into the house. "Liz? Liz?" Bob yelled in his deep voice. There was no answer. In the distance I heard the wail of sirens. I knew we should wait before going any further, but we couldn't do it. Ray pounded up behind us. As though in tacit agreement we practically tiptoed further into the house. There was no sign of Liz in the living or dining room. We made our way through the kitchen onto the patio. Ray started toward the pool but stopped short by the barbecue. "My God!" he whispered.

Liz lay on her back, a red stain spreading across her chest. The handle of a knife protruded from below her heart. She had changed from the shorts and halter top she had worn for the party into the caftan I saw her wearing a few days before. Next to her a small table lay on its side, two glasses and a wine bottle broken beside it. Ray dropped to his knees and tentatively reached for Liz's wrist and then for her neck. I heard Bob begin to retch. He dashed forward and threw up in the pool.

I heard others approaching rapidly and then we seemed to be

surrounded by a sea of blue. "Step aside, Sir!" a voice ordered. Like an automaton Ray rose to his feet. He came to stand next to Bob and me. I wanted to look away as paramedics bent over Liz's prostrate form but I couldn't. My body started to shake uncontrollably and I heard my breath coming in deep sobs. Ray put his arm round my waist and Bob reached for my hand. It seemed to take hours rather than minutes for the paramedics to regain their feet. One of them, a short Latina, shook her head sharply at a police officer. She and her partner wheeled their empty gurney toward the front door. Clearly this was a crime scene. A lot had to be done before Liz would make the trip to the morgue. Through a fog I heard a deep voice barking orders. Without being bidden Ray, Bob and I followed the paramedics. As they reached the door I heard Lexie screaming again for her mother. She ran toward the house but Marcia, who was surprisingly strong, grabbed her and forcibly turned her away, murmuring into her ear.

Marcia eased Lexie onto a bench on the house's front porch. Linda knelt in front of her, gently rubbing her hands. Bernice stood in her yard, arms wrapped around herself as though she were cold. When she saw Ray she hurried over. She threw her arms around him and they held each other tightly, her face pressed against his shoulder. After a moment she looked up at him, a question in her eyes. "I'm all right," he assured her. Bernice seemed undecided as to what to do. "Go home and stay with the kids," she told Ray finally. "I'll be home as soon as I can but right now I need to be with Lexie." Ray nodded and trudged across the street, head bent. Bernice positioned herself so that Lexie was sandwiched between Marcia and herself.

Nick sidled over to me. "Mom?" he asked tentatively, his wide eyes staring out of a pale face.

"Mrs. Williams is dead, honey," I said after taking a ragged breath.

"But how?" he asked. "Did she have a heart attack or something?" I shook my head silently, fearing that if I tried to speak I would follow Bob's example and throw up. His eyes widened further. "Then what?"

The ambulance pulled slowly away. As it did, a man wearing a jacket and tie approached the uniformed officers. As he spoke with them his eyes kept flickering in Lexie's direction. As I watched him I moved toward her and my friends until I was standing behind the bench. Nick moved with me. "Nick, please go home."

"But Mom," he protested.

"Go. Now." I said. "Don't text or call any of your friends. Stay in the house. Or if you want you can go to Max's." Nick gestured toward Max and Bill and very slowly they moved away.

"What if Lexie needs us?" He turned and made one last effort to stay.

"Right now she has all the support she needs. I appreciate your thought. She'll need you later for sure." I studied his stricken face. "I'll come and get you if she wants you to be with her," I said gently. "I promise."

The boys headed in the direction of my house. Apparently, there was security in numbers.

The man I had been watching approached Lexie with a policewoman in tow. He surprised me by crouching down in front of her rather than towering over the bench. The policewoman stood unobtrusively to one side. "Lexie?" he said in a soft voice. "I'm Detective Furman." Lexie stared at him, eyes swollen, face blotchy from crying. "Can you tell me what happened tonight?"

"I went to the park to see the fireworks," she whispered. "A bunch of us kids went." He nodded encouragingly. "When I came home I called my mom but she didn't answer." Her eyes welled with tears. "She didn't want to go to the fireworks. She was going to finish cleaning up after our party."

"Liz had a neighborhood barbecue," I volunteered. The detective looked at me assessingly, gray eyes sharp and inquisitive.

"And you are?"

"Jackie Olsen. I live next door." He nodded and shifted his attention back to Lexie.

"She would have told me if she was going out," Lexie declared. "I knew she was home. I thought maybe she was on the patio because you can't hear when someone yells from the front of the house. She always tells me that." Lexie began to sob again. " I mean she always told me that." The policewoman handed Marcia a blanket. Marcia gently wrapped it around Lexie's shoulders. Next came, of all things, a Teddy bear, which Lexie grabbed and clutched to herself like a life preserver. "So I went out to the pool and that's when I saw her. She was just lying there and she didn't answer me. There was all that blood...and I...I couldn't see her breathing. I just screamed and I ran." Bernice's arms were wrapped tightly around the girl. "That's enough!" she said sharply.

The detective held his hands out placatingly and rose. "Is there someone we should call?" he asked.

I nodded. "Her father, if he's in town." The detective raised a questioning eyebrow. "His job takes him away from home a lot. And he and Liz are...were...separated." He nodded again.

The detective got Dan's number from Bob, who was still standing to one side of our tableau and turned away to dial. I strained to hear his end of the conversation but only heard the rumble of his low voice. Suddenly I was exhausted. I dropped down on the stairs and put my head on my knees. Someone threw a blanket around my shoulders. I looked up. "You've had quite a shock," Detective Furman said.

"I've never seen a dead person before," I said. He looked sympathetic. "And there was so much blood, and the knife..." I closed my eyes.

"Do you want a Teddy bear?" he asked. I looked up, uncertain as to whether he was being sarcastic.

"She doesn't need a Teddy bear; she has her friends and we're better than any stuffed animal." Linda plopped onto the stairs close beside me.

"Then she's lucky." The detective flashed a brief smile. He turned as Dan's car pulled into the driveway. "Please don't leave until the officers have taken your statement." He turned back around. "Oh, and Mrs. Olsen?"

I looked up.

"Since you were in the house I'd like your shoes, please."
"My shoes?"
"In case you stepped in anything in the house we can tell your foot prints from anyone else's."
My stomach churned. I snatched my favorite sandals off my feet and handed them to him. I suspected I'd never wear them again.
"And we'll take your fingerprints. Same reason." He walked away.
I sighed. It was going to be a long night. And in spite of what Linda said I really did want that Teddy bear.
During our conversation Dan had sprung from his car and hastened to his daughter. Lexie jumped to her feet, ran to him and threw herself into his arms. He held her tightly, stroking her hair, whispering into her ear. Her sobs subsided and Dan looked around in bewilderment. "What's going on? Where's Liz? Has she had an accident?" He spied Linda and me sitting on the steps. "The message I got didn't make sense. Did something happen to her?"
Detective Furman had been watching the scene impassively. Now he stepped forward. "Mr. Williams," he said, "I'm sorry to inform you that your wife has been murdered." What a job he had! I couldn't imagine delivering such a message, never mind delivering it with out a single touch of emotion.
Dan reacted as though he'd been punched. "What do you mean murdered? How? When? Who? Where?" He seemed to be reeling from the blow.
"She's in the house, Daddy," Lexie said, still clinging to him. "I found her."
"Oh my God, Lexie!" He pulled her closer and buried his face in her hair. His shoulders were shaking.
A man in uniform approached the detective. "What do you have for me, Wes?" the detective asked.
"Not much yet, sir," he replied. "But I can tell you there's no sign of forced entry." Furman acknowledged his remark with a quick nod. "We're going to be a long time, Sir," the officer said. "Apparently the deceased had a big party and there's lots of stuff to collect. It's going to be a bear to sort out."

"Thanks, Wes. Keep me posted." He had been watching Dan and Lexie as he talked with the officer. He continued to watch impassively until Dan looked up, having somewhat gotten control of his emotions.

"Mr. Williams," the detective said, "Where were you this evening?"

"I was with my sister and her family. They had a cookout," Dan replied. He stood up straight and shot a sharp look at Furman. "Why are you asking me this?" The detective didn't reply. "My God, man, surely you don't think *I* had anything to do with Liz's murder?"

"I'm just gathering information, sir."

"Well, you can gather it through my attorney!" Dan yelled. "My daughter just found her mother's body and you're questioning me like I'm a common criminal? I'm not answering any more questions without my lawyer being present and neither is Lexie. We're leaving."

"Before you go, let us have an address and phone number where we can reach you."

"You can't hold us here!" Dan said, incredulous. "After what my daughter's been through, she needs to get away from this place."

"Actually, I *can* hold you," Furman said evenly, "but I'd rather not. If you give us your address and phone number you can be on your way."

"Are you sure you don't want to check me for blood first?" Dan said sarcastically.

"We will be requesting DNA samples from both of you," the detective said. "That information could be used against you, and you may want to consult with an attorney before complying."

Dan stared at him. "This is unbelievable. The address is 4200 Richfield Lane, Apartment 102. My attorney is Hannah Lee. And we are leaving." He turned. ignoring the rest of us, escorted Lexie to his car, gently helped her into the passenger seat, got in behind the wheel and took off, tires squealing.

My friends and I stared open mouthed.

Furman turned to us. "Now, about those statements."

Man, what a night. Teddy bears all around please.

CHAPTER SIX

Mercifully the boys were asleep by the time I dragged myself home. Nick was sprawled on the sofa, one arm drooped over the side, the other covering his forehead. He snored rhythmically. Maggie was splayed on his chest, the top of her head touching his chin. She wagged her stub of a tail when she saw me but otherwise didn't move. Her body moved up and down in time to Nick's breathing.

Max and Bill had dragged out the blow-up mattresses we used for camping and were sound asleep on the living room floor. The cat, not always the most empathetic creature, had curled up behind Max's knees. She blinked slowly at me but made no attempt to leave her position.

I tiptoed around them and softly closed the door to my bedroom. Briefly I thought about going back to the kitchen and pouring myself a stiff drink, but decided that wasn't appealing. For a moment the bathtub beckoned, but I rejected that option also. I quickly brushed my teeth and put on my pajamas. I expected sleep to elude me, but I was wrong.

The sun was streaming into my bedroom when I awoke. I stumbled to the kitchen to find a note from Nick. The neighborhood teens were gathering at Bernice and Ray's home. I sent up a guilty and heartfelt prayer of thanks that my friends were dealing with the initial fallout from the previous night's events. I hoped designating that task didn't make me a bad mother.

I had just showered and was slapping on lipstick (why I was doing that I couldn't tell you; I rarely wear makeup at home) when the doorbell rang. I peered through the side light and spotted Detective Furman standing at my door. It looked like he was systematically deadheading the petunias in my porch flower containers, something I had been meaning to do for several days.

I made a mental note to be more proactive. Maybe I would even wash the kitchen floor and dust my office and...For Heaven's sake, where were these thoughts coming from? I wasn't a perfect housekeeper by any means, but the house looked fine. Why was I worrying about these things now? Was I concerned about what a policeman I just met would think? Ridiculous. Get a grip, Jackie. Apparently, the man is a neat freak. Who cares?

When I opened the door the detective held out a handful of wilted blossoms with a sheepish smile. "Sorry," he said. "I couldn't help myself."

Instinctively I accepted the proffered contribution.

"Mrs. Olsen?" he asked, flashing his badge and identification card, "I'd like to talk with you about last night. Is now a good time?"

I nodded wordlessly and led the way to the living room, tossing the spent blossoms in the trash along the way.

The detective took in the details of the living room before sitting down. "Nice house," he commented.

"Thanks, we like it," I replied.

"Is Mr. Olsen home?" he asked.

"I'm a widow."

He blushed. "I should have known that. I'm sorry." He opened a file folder and scanned the papers it contained. I studied him surreptitiously, pretending to be distracted by a magazine open on the table in front of me. He was a good-looking man, some might say handsome, with dark hair turning silver at the temples, a firm jaw and a straight, Romanesque nose. This morning he looked tired, bluish circles under his eyes, a stubble turning his cheeks and jaw purple. He shifted position and muscles rippled under his freshly laundered shirt.

"Would you like some coffee?" I asked.

He moved his gaze toward me and smiled, a crooked smile that caused a dimple to form on one side of his mouth. Those gray eyes I had noticed the night before, almost silver with flecks of darker gray, framed by luxurious black eyelashes any woman would envy, crinkled briefly.

"No, thank you. I'm already highly caffeinated and the day is young," he replied. "What I'd like to do is start by going over your statement from last night." He took me meticulously through what I had told the police officer who questioned me, asking questions that sought to illuminate my answers. I was amazed at how many ways he could ask the same question. Really, I thought, I need to take note of this for use in my books. After a while, however, his questioning became annoying. "Do you do this with every witness?" I finally asked in exasperation.

"Do what?" he asked.

"Ask every question a hundred different ways."

"Do I do that?"

"You know you do," I said. "And you answer questions with another question."

"Sorry." Clearly he wasn't sorry at all.

He continued his interrogation. Time marched on. After a while surely even he could tell I had nothing to add.

"So you didn't go to the fireworks last night?" he asked.

"No."

"And you didn't stay outside your house to watch?"

"No." I explained Maggie's fear of the noise. At the sound of her name Maggie raised her head and gave a huge yawn.

Detective Furman leaned over and gave her a head rub. "Scary, wasn't it pup?" he said. Maggie gave his hand a sloppy kiss and he smiled.

The detective sat a moment, contemplating his notes. Then his eyes met mine directly and my heart gave a little leap.

"Were you and Mrs. Williams friends?" he asked.

I thought. Were Liz and I friends? He sat silently, eying my every move.

"Were Liz and I friends?" I repeated. He waited. "I'm not avoiding the question," I said, "It's not something I've really thought about." Still he waited.

"When our children were younger," I finally said, "We were closer. I suspect it's natural to be drawn together when you have little kids." He nodded. "But more recently we had very different situations. I'm trying to raise a teenaged boy on my own and believe me, it's not easy." He nodded again encouragingly. "Don't get me wrong. Nick's a great kid, but he needs a dad and I always expected his father to be here." Damn it, why was I telling him this anyway? I felt tears forming and blinked my eyes furiously. For goodness' sake, I was *not* going to make a fool of myself and cry in front of this man. The detective pretended not to notice my wet eyes. "Anyway, these days I'm learning how to unclog toilets and change air filters and keep the pump on the darned fish pond running. Liz was busy decorating her house and going shopping. I'm sure you noticed how gorgeous her house is."

"A bit perfect for my taste," he said. "I like this better." I studied him. Was he trying to make me feel good, thinking he'd soften me up? But what would he want to do that for? I straightened my spine. Surely I wasn't a suspect! I'd read my share of mysteries. I wrote the darned things. And I watched plenty of cop shows and knew how sneaky detectives could be, luring you into false complacency and then jolting you into a confession. Actually, I didn't know any of this first hand, but that's how things went in my fictional world. I vowed to be vigilant and circumspect.

"Where did Mrs. Williams get her money?" Furman asked. Well, that certainly came out of left field.

"I don't have the slightest idea. I've always assumed it came from her husband."

"She didn't work outside the home?"

"Not for a long as I've known her, and that's been a long time."

He made a note. "What can you tell me about Mr. Williams?"

"I'm sure you know where he lives and works," I said. "I don't know what you're looking for."

"What's he like? Does he have a temper? Is he quiet? Is he rowdy? What kind of father and husband is he?"

"Why are you asking me these things?" I said. "I don't know what you want from me."

He leaned back, twirling his pen. "It's important that I understand the character of everyone close to Mrs. Williams. As a longtime neighbor surely you have some opinions."

I thought back to Ray's comments at the party. I decided I wasn't about to share those. Let the detective get his feelings from Ray if he could.

"I've always liked Dan," I said cautiously. "I've never seen him angry or upset unless his favorite team was losing, and even then he'd only use a few choice words. Nothing different from the other men I know." The detective made a note. "He has a good paying job and I've always assumed him to be a good provider. He does travel a lot, and Liz complained about that from time to time. When he was home, though, he seemed to make an effort to spend time with his family."

"Why did they separate?"

I pondered the question. "Liz seemed to change over the past year. She didn't seem interested in doing family things as much as she had been. She seemed to be spending a lot more and going out a lot more than she had. I think she and Dan grew apart and finally he got fed up with her running all over the place and not paying attention to him."

"And Lexie?"

Warning! Warning! Landmine ahead. "What do you mean?"

"Did they get along?"

I decided to tread carefully. "As much as teenaged daughters and mothers generally do, I suppose."

He looked at me closely. "How did they get along after the separation?"

Oh, drat. "Lexie adores her father. She's been upset."

"Did she blame her mother?" Boy, was he sharp.

"Probably so."

The detective allowed a half smile to show on his face. "I understand you want be loyal to your friends," he said. "But I need to understand the lay of the land and that means you need to be honest with me."

I sighed. "Recently she'd been pretty upset with her mother." He made a note

"Do you consider your son and Lexie to be friends?"

I sat up straight. Where was this going? "Yes. They've grown up together."

"Any possibility they're more than friends?"

"Not that I know of." I told him the story about the ex-boyfriend and the cheerleader. He shook his head. "Tough age."

"So Lexie and Nick went to the fireworks together?" he asked.

"They went with a group of friends."

"Did they stay together the whole time?"

"I don't know. I wasn't there. You'd have to ask Nick."

"Did they return together?"

"I think so but I didn't seem them immediately when they came back." He made a note. Another note. I wondered what he was picking up on. Knowing that, really understanding how a detective thinks would really help my writing. What was wrong with me? How could I think about that in the middle of an interrogation (assuming that's what this was)?

A terrifying thought ran through my brain. "You can't possibly think Lexie had anything to do with her mother's murder?"

The detective capped his pen. "I'm just trying to understand the players," he said.

I picked at my nail polish, something I do only when I'm nervous.

"I understand you're a writer," Furman said.

I nodded.

"What kinds of books do you write?"

"Mysteries," I muttered.

Here it comes. He's going to laugh.

"Mysteries?" he asked.

"Cozy mysteries," I said. "Think Agatha Christie."

I waited for the laughter but it didn't come. Instead, he nodded. "My niece is crazy about those books," he said. "Every major occasion she has a list she wants me to buy from." He named some well-known authors. I wasn't on the list, but maybe I could give him a couple books to see if that would change.

"Maybe I should give her of couple of your books," he said, smiling. Was the man a mind reader?

"I have some copies you could have."

"Thanks. I'd like that." Our eyes met and my heart did that little fluttery thing again.
"Tell me more about the Williamses," he said.
I found myself telling him about Liz's days as a stage mother, her separation from Dan, the rumors about her involvement with other men, the red sports car. I didn't tell him about Lexie and the college boys. I felt the need to keep Lexie's confidence if I could.
"Who do you think killed her?" the detective asked, leaning forward.
"I don't have the slightest idea," I said.
"I understand the divorce was pretty acrimonious."
"I wouldn't know." I felt like we were going round in circles again.
"You and Mrs. Williams didn't talk about it?"
"No."
"Seems kind of funny, you having been neighbors for so long."
"Some things are personal," I said.
"Did you talk to Mr. Williams about it?"
"I haven't talked to him since he left."
"Did you talk to him about it before he left?"
"No." The fluttery feeling was changing. I recognized it clearly for what it was. Anxiety. I had been thinking of Detective Furman as a friendly labrador. Now I realized he was a bulldog.
"Has Mr. Williams kept in touch with anyone else in the neighborhood?" the detective asked.
I thought back again to my conversation with Ray at the party. The detective's eyes were boring into mine. Reluctantly I gave him Ray's name. He nodded curtly and stood. "I'm going to want to talk to your son also," he said.
"Nick? Whatever for?" I asked.
"I'm going to talk to all of Lexie's friends."
"He doesn't know anything."
"Come now, Mrs. Olsen," The detective raised an eyebrow. "Surely you're not going to tell me a sixteen-year-old boy tells his mother everything?"

"You can't talk with him unless I'm there." I crossed my arms over my chest. My foot started tapping of its own volition.
"That goes without saying." He fished a business card out of his wallet and laid it on the coffee table. "Call me if you think of anything. Anything at all. Ask for Riley."
I remained glued to the couch.
"I'll see myself out." The detective flashed his dimpled smile. As he opened the door he hesitated. "In those books you write," he said, "there's usually some amateur who decides to solve the crime because the cops are too stupid or lazy or incompetent ... whatever. I hope you don't confuse your books with real life." He closed the door.
I remained sitting, slack jawed. I had been wrong earlier. The man wasn't a bull dog; he was a pit bull.
The door opened again. "Oh, and your petunias could use some water."
Jerk.

CHAPTER SEVEN

The following day brought a threat of rain. I stood at the window, watching dark clouds gather in the distance as the wind picked up as a harbinger of a storm to come. The police were still working next door. I couldn't imagine what was taking so long, party or no. Nick was still home. He continued to be upset over Liz's death. Lexie wasn't answering her phone or texts, and that had him completely on edge. I had decided to let him stay out of school for one more day, but insisted that he clean his room before he could hang out with his other friends who had also been granted a reprieve. The darned room looked and smelled like a sports locker and I couldn't take it any longer. I didn't understand how he could stand to leave his room like that when he refused to leave the house unless he smelled like the cologne counter at Macy's, every hair was in place and his clothes were clean and well put together. Teenaged boys are strange creatures.

Maggie was dozing on the cat's bed, her puppy frame curled into a tiny ball, while the cat had once again taken over the larger bed we had bought for Maggie. Interesting power dynamic. I made a note to buy matching beds so the poor puppy wouldn't have to contort herself like a pretzel in order to have something soft on which to sleep.

The phone rang. "Have you heard the police want to interview the kids this morning?"

Bernice didn't bother to identify herself. She sounded stressed out and I could imagine her running her fingers through her hair until it stood out like a Frankenstein wig.

"No, I haven't heard anything," I replied.

"They wanted to do it at the school but Ray told them no," she said. "He said there are already too many rumors circulating. Some of the kids are so upset and scared that he's brought in Ed

Scruggs to serve as an additional counselor."

"My goodness. Ray has a lot on his plate. He certainly doesn't need the police to contend with on top of everything else."

"That's what he said. So Detective Furman said they'd bring everyone into the police station. Talk about threatening! Now my phone won't stop ringing. All the moms are calling me and freaking out. I don't know why they're calling me and I don't know what to tell them. It's not like their kids are being arrested, for Heaven's sake." I heard her take a breath. It was totally out of character for Bernice to be this frazzled. I knew I had to come up with a compromise for the location of the interviews. For a split second I thought about offering my house as a venue and then realized what a stupid move that would be. I couldn't imagine my living room packed with nervous or excited teens and their hysterical parents.

"Let's think about this a minute," I said. "How about the recreation center? There are some rooms there that could be used. Or maybe the meeting rooms at the library?"

"Those are both great ideas," Bernice replied. "I don't know why I didn't think of it. My brain just froze. Let me give Janice at the library a call and see what she can do."

I hung up and thought for a while about my interview with Riley Furman the previous day. He was an expert interrogator, no doubt about that. I knew Nick wasn't a suspect and we had nothing to worry about. Nonetheless, I decided to give my husband's former law partner a call.

"My goodness, Jackie, what in the world is going on in your neighborhood? I can't believe your next-door neighbor was murdered. Are you all right?" I smiled as I pictured Jeremy Barber, head shaved, dark mustache neatly curled, wearing a $1,000 suit and imitating Kojak by sucking on a lollypop.

I confirmed that we were fine and filled him in about my interview the previous day. "Go on," he said.

"The police are interviewing Nick and his friends today. Should he have a lawyer with him?'

"Is there any reason to think he had any involvement with this

murder?"
"Absolutely none."
"Are you aware of any illegal activities he's involved in?"
"Same answer."
"That's what I figured. Then no, there's no need for counsel. Tell you what, though. If at any time you become uncomfortable with the questioning you stop it, call me and I'll come sit in."
"Thanks, Jeremy. I'm sure I won't be calling, but knowing you're here makes me feel better."
There was a brief pause. "I'll always be here for you and Nick. You know that. By the way, Mary and I were talking about you just the other day. She's going to call and arrange dinner. There's a new Mediterranean place that's gotten rave reviews."
"Sounds great. I'm looking forward to it." I hung up the phone feeling much more relaxed.
Nick's interview was scheduled for 11:00. The town librarian had come through with meeting rooms. We arrived slightly before our appointment time and approached an officer seated at a folding table with several sheets of names in front of him.
"Name?"
"Nick Olsen," my son replied shakily. The officer checked off his name. "No talking. No phone calls, no texting, no emailing. If I see you using a portable device I will confiscate it. Is that clear?"
"Yes, sir."
The officer glanced at me. "That goes for your mother. Do you understand, Ma'am?"
What was I, stupid? "Yes."
He looked once more at his list. "You are scheduled to be interviewed by Detective Furman. We'll call you when he's ready."
Oh joy, oh rapture. A repeat performance of the day before. I could hardly wait. At least I had an idea of how the interview would go, so that was a plus. We took our places with other students and their waiting parents. Nick performed fist bumps with some of the boys. We parents smiled at each other encouragingly. I watched the fathers who were present and longed for my husband. I spotted Teddy, the college boy Anna had been

with, and waved my fingers at him. He gave a small smile and inclined his head slightly.

At last Nick's name was called and we joined Riley Furman in an interview room. At first he was polite and somewhat perfunctory, stating our names and the time and location of the interview. He asked Nick some general questions about himself. What were his hobbies? What was his favorite food? Did he like a particular sports team? What was he going to do this summer? The questions were designed, I suppose, to put Nick somewhat at ease. It seemed to work. For some reason they made me more uncomfortable and alert. Once they had established they were both die hard Nationals fans and liked pepperoni pizza the real questioning began.

"Tell me about your relationship with Lexie Williams," Furman said.

Nick seemed taken aback. "What do you mean? We've known each other practically our whole lives."

"So would you say you're friends?"

"Yes."

"Boyfriend and girlfriend?"

Nick looked as if he didn't really understand the question. "Lexie and me? Nah, we're just friends."

"Does Lexie have a boyfriend?"

"She did but they broke up." Once again the detective heard the story of the unfaithful Rob.

I was beginning to get restless. "Is there a point to these questions?" I asked.

Riley glanced at me. "There is." He turned back to Nick. "Tell me about Lexie's relationship with her parents."

Nick looked at me. "Go ahead," I said. "If Detective Furman thinks it's important it must be."

"Lexie's really close with her dad," Nick said. "Before her parents separated she spent a lot of time with him. He was one of the swim team coaches, so that was cool. He's away a lot – he works for a big pharmaceutical company – and she was happy when he was home."

"What about after her parents split up?"
Nick looked at me again, and I nodded encouragingly.
"She didn't get to see her dad as much as she wanted. She told me she was going to go to his lawyer and make her tell the judge she wanted to spend more time with him."
That was news to me.
"And did she?"
"No."
"Do you know why not?"
"I'm not sure, but I think she was afraid of what her mother would do." He paused. "I think she thought it would hurt her mother's feelings, too and she felt bad about that."
"Was Lexie getting along with her mother after her parents separated?"
"Sometimes. But a lot of the time she was really mad at her. She said she kept going out when Lexie wanted her to stay home and she wouldn't let her see her dad when she wanted to. Her parents fought a lot and it really upset her."
"Was her dad at the house when they fought?"
"Sometimes, but it was mostly on the phone. One time they were fighting so hard Lexie ran over to our house and kind of hid in my room."
She did? Where had I been? Maybe the detective was correct. Teenaged boys didn't tell their mothers everything.
"Was she afraid it was getting violent?"
"Yeah. It never had before, but she said they were threatening each other with all sorts of things."
"Such as?"
"He threatened to take Lexie. He said he'd tell the court her mother was an unfit parent. Her mother said she'd take every dime he had and he'd end up in the poor house."
How awful. I wished I had known how much Lexie was going through.
"Ultimately, though, Lexie didn't try to move in with her dad?"
"No. He thought she should live with her grandparents so she wouldn't have to be in the middle of everything, but her grand-

mother's really strict and Lexie wasn't sure she'd let her see her mother because she didn't like her so she didn't want to."

It took me a while to unravel the grammar. Finally, I got it. Dan's mother didn't like Liz. I hadn't realized that.

"Tell me about the night of the party?"

"What about it?"

"What did you do? What did you observe?"

Nick thought a moment. "We went over to Lexie's house about 4. Me and..." I couldn't resist. I frowned. In return Riley frowned in my direction. "Some of the other kids and I played water sports." Then Riley got it. The house of grammar correction. Briefly his dimple appeared. "Then we helped put the food out and ate and just hung out." Nick finished.

There you go, four hours condensed to three sentences. Aren't teenagers wonderful?

"What did you do after you ate?"

"We went to the park to watch the fireworks."

"Who went with you? "

Nick ticked off names on his fingers. "Max, Lexie, Bill, Bill's brother, Teddy and Anna."

"Did Mrs. Williams go?"

"No. She said she was going to clean up and watch the fireworks from her house."

"Did she usually go?"

Nick scrunched up his nose trying to remember previous years. "Yeah. She really liked fireworks." My eyes teared as I recalled Liz tilting back her head, her oohs and aahs as loud as anyone's. "My mother usually goes, too, but she told me Maggie got scared and she decided to stay with her."

The detective nodded. He knew this already. "What about the other adults at the party?"

"I'm not really sure," Nick admitted. "Max's parents went, but he drove with us because he had plans to meet up with his girl-friend."

Max had a girlfriend? I must have looked nonplussed because Furman slid his eyes in my direction and one corner of his mouth ticked upward.

"Did the rest of you stay together?"

"No. Teddy and Anna decided they wanted ice cream. He had his own car so he said he'd drive Anna home and they split off." Ice cream? After everything they'd just eaten? How do kids do that?

"And the rest of you?"

"Lexie took off with some of the girls from the tennis team. I saw a girl I like and we decided to watch the fireworks together. I don't know what Bill and his brother did." Nick liked a girl? What girl? This was news to me. The detective's mouth did that upward tick thing again. If he laughed I'd deck him.

I pulled my mind back to the questioning. Uh oh. I thought Lexie stayed with Nick and the other kids from our street. Unless we found people she was with the whole evening was she without an alibi? Nick may have just thrown Lexie under the bus without realizing it. But he had to tell the truth, no matter where it led.

"What did you do after the fireworks were over?"

"We all met back at my car. Well, Mom's car. I drove home."

"Was Lexie with you?"

"Yes."

"What happened after you got home?"

"We were pretty tired. Lexie went into her house. The rest of us were hanging around, talking in the driveway. Max and Bill were going to spend the night at our house." They were? News to me. Oh dear, this was not good. Clearly, I was not nearly as on top of things as I had thought.

"We were just heading in when Lexie ran out and started screaming." Nick sat back in his seat, looking exhausted.

"Is there anything else you want to tell me, Nick?"

"Like what?"

"Anything at all."

"No."

"All right, then. This interview is terminated." The detective stated the time and turned off the recording device. "Thank you for coming in." He started to rise.

"How do you do what you do?" I asked.

He sat back down. "I don't understand what you mean."

I made a sweeping gesture. "This job. All this interviewing and sifting through things. Last night – the blood, the chaos, that scene with Dan. It just seems awful to me."

"I didn't cause the confrontation last night," he said. "But it was informative."

"Do you seriously consider Dan a suspect?"

"Damn right I do."

"But he's..."

"What?" Riley snapped. "He's so nice? He loves his daughter? He coached the swim team? So what? Do you think all murderers are raving lunatics? You write mysteries for a living. In your books isn't the killer often the nice person next door? Or down the street?"

I couldn't disagree.

Nick was sitting rigidly upright, his fists clenched and his face tense. "Is Lexie a suspect?"

"Hell ...excuse me,"Riley said, glancing at me, "Heck, yes."

"She can't be!" Nick cried. "She's the kindest person in the world! She won't even squash a bug."

"Kids don't kill their parents? It doesn't happen often, but it does. Think of the Menendez brothers."

Nick looked stricken. Furman studied his face and seemed to take pity on him. He leaned forward slightly and clasped his hands on the table in front of him. "In cases like this, family members are always suspects. This is particularly true when people are going through a nasty divorce. These are the first people we look at. It doesn't mean that's where we stop looking and it doesn't mean we assume they're guilty."

Nick still appeared upset.

The detective examined his hands for a moment and then looked up. "Here's the way I see my job. I'm a voice for the victim. It might be a murder victim, it might be someone who's been mugged, it might be an old lady whose life savings have been swindled away. Sometimes I'm the only voice. It's my job to find the truth. And to do that I will look everywhere I need to; I will lift every rock to see what crawls out from under it, I will examine every fact and if there's a puzzle I will work with the pieces until they fit."

He switched his attention to me. "I'm looking for facts. I don't go on hunches or intuition, although sometimes those can lead to an important fact. My team and I do honest, by the book police work. Hopefully at the end of the day, we do find that truth we're looking for. Sometimes we don't and that can prey on you for a lifetime." His eyes clouded for a moment. I suspected he was remembering a case or two. "But when we nail someone for a crime, when we see justice served, it's all worth it.

"Right now I'm Liz Williams' voice. I don't know who killed her, but I'm going to do my darndest to find out. This afternoon I'm going to the morgue and I'm going to watch the coroner cut open the body of a beautiful woman who should have had many more years to live. Any more questions?"

"Are we suspects?" Nick asked. "I mean Mom and me."

Riley smiled. "No. Not at the moment. I think you're nice people who are loyal friends and deeply care about people. The world would be better if there were more people like you." He held up a finger. "However. If in the course of my investigation I find a fact that points to you as being guilty, I will come after you and I will come after you hard."

Nick gulped.

The detective smiled, realizing he may have scared Nick more than necessary. "I'm confident that's not going to happen. You need to relax and maybe introduce your mother to that girl, whoever she is."

Nick smiled. "Maybe," he said.

"One more question," I said.

Riley glanced at his watch. "A quick one. I'm running late."

"Who's your favorite fictional detective?"

He was clearly surprised. "Let me think. When I was kid, I loved Columbo. But these days I'd have to say Tom Barnaby in the Midsomer series."

I was surprised. "Why?"

"He's a good man, he doesn't give up, he plays by the book and he follows the facts." He smiled. "The crimes are really gruesome and I can't imagine having that many psychotic murderers in such a small area, but I admire his character. Sometimes he's a little slow on the uptake. That's my only criticism. There are too many last-minute rescues of people trapped with raving lunatics."

He rose and shook our hands. "Thanks for coming in."

As he walked us to the door he said, "Do you want to know my least fictional detective?"

"Absolutely."

"Jessica Fletcher. I've never seen a woman get herself in more stupid situations in my life." I smiled. I had to agree. I loved the old show, but she sure did some stupid things.

Nick was quiet on the way out of the building and as we headed out of the parking lot.

"Penny for your thoughts?"

He shook his head.

I waited a while. "How about some lunch?"

"Dinah's Diner?" he said looking at me hopefully.

Dinah's Diner. Home of the half pound chili cheese jalapeno burger. It was a complete dietary disaster, particularly if paired with a milkshake. But if that's what it took to shake Nick out of his reverie and into communication, Dinah's Diner it was.

At the diner we placed our orders. Nick of course ordered the calorific extravaganza. I ordered a chef's salad with the understanding that I could have some of his onion rings.

"Spill," I said after his milkshake arrived. I was virtuously drinking unsweetened iced tea, but was eying the small portion of milkshake still in the icy metal container in which it has been prepared.

"It might be really cool to be a police detective."

I practically choked on an ice cube. "What happened to engineering and Cal Tech? You've said that's what you wanted since you were in middle school."

"I know, but I'm re-thinking. After all Detective Furman told us

I have to reconsider. I mean, being a voice for people like Liz. It's really important."

"Don't romanticize the job." I cautioned. "It's hard work, You see terrible things and deal with awful people. The hours are long, the pay isn't great, it's hard to have a family life..."

"Maybe forensic science. That sounds fascinating."

Oh, dear. I hoped Nick hadn't found a new idol. I much preferred it when it was Albert Einstein, as much as I admired what Riley said.

Nick took a bite of his burger.

"So," I said, changing the subject. "Who's this girl?"

He just smiled.

CHAPTER EIGHT

After Nick and I were back home I wandered dispiritedly through the house. I put the dirty dishes in the dishwasher and threw in a load of wash. I found myself in my study, staring down at the neatly stacked pages of plot outline. The detective's sarcastic parting words the previous day came back to me, 'some amateur decides to solve the crime...' I thought about our conversation this morning, his passion for his job. He was right, I decided. At least on some level he was. So many mystery novelists delighted in showing the police as incompetent or worse. All the mysteries I read, along with the ones I wrote, were contrived. Even Miss Marple was at her core nothing more than a nosy busybody.

Why in the world would someone other than a detective try to solve a murder? Or even want to? All the reasons I had come up with, or that other authors had set forth, seemed feeble. And the harm an amateur could do suddenly seemed so apparent.

Unexpected tears dropped onto the papers, smearing the words. Why did I have to write with a fountain pen anyway? I brushed the tears off my cheeks. In one sentence yesterday Riley Furman had burse my happy little writing bubble. Damn him! I couldn't write now. I wasn't sure I would ever do it again.

'Oh, stop the pity party!' I told myself. 'So you write escape fiction. So you like to read mysteries. What's wrong with that?' I raised my head defiantly. I straightened the papers on my desk, even though they didn't need it. I was going to make this the best book I'd ever written. My amateur was going to solve the crime. She was going to get her man, too. This wasn't real life; it was fiction and it would be fun to read. Let Riley Furman figure out who killed Liz Williams. I'd leave him to it. My amateur would win the day, and my readers would have fun while she did it. But first I was going to pick some tomatoes before it rained.

Our normally quiet cul-de-sac was busier than I could remember it ever being. Even neighbors we rarely saw had found reasons to be in their yards. And the dog walkers! My goodness, where did they all come from? Maggie would have barked herself hoarse had she been home. I just hoped these people would pick up after their pets. Yep, one just went in Marcia's yard. She'd have a fit if… oh, good, out came a little plastic bag.

Strangers rode by on their bikes, coasting and craning their necks as they passed the Williams' house. Power walkers walked less powerfully than normal. 'Bad news really does fascinate us' I thought. 'No wonder the news is so full of it.'

Personally, I had stopped watching the local news and even most national news shows eons ago. Our town of Summer Hill, Virginia was generally peaceful, but if one bad thing happened, it exploded onto the television. I wondered what the local media was making of Liz's death. Sure enough, there was a media van with a pretty little thing talking into a microphone in front of the Williams house. 'Bubble-headed bleach blonde' the Eagles would have said. I had to admit, watching her, that I was curious. In spite of my reservations I would watch the news tonight. Maybe I could stomach it if accompanied by a snack and an adult beverage.

At the house police personnel came and went, each concentrating on his or her role in the drama. I spotted Riley Furman talking with an attractive Latina with a gold shield clipped to her belt. The heat and humidity were getting the better of him. The shirt that had been freshly laundered that morning was beginning to stick to him, outlining a flat abdomen and well-developed pectoral muscles, along with sinewy arms and...WOW! He saw me staring and scowled. At least I thought he scowled, but he could have been squinting, trying to see more clearly. I thought about scowling in return, but gave him my sweetest smile instead. He continued scowling, or squinting, whichever. I wriggled my fingers at him. A uniformed officer approached him and he turned away.

A slight movement caught my eye. Dan Williams was standing under a large tulip poplar at the edge of his yard, closely watching the police. I walked over. What do you say? 'I'm sorry for your loss' seemed so trite.

"What a mess." That probably wasn't much better.

"No kidding." He slid his eyes toward me for a moment.

"How are you holding up?"

He shrugged. "As well as can be expected."

"How's Lexie! Where is she?"

"She's doing terrible. She keeps saying this wouldn't have happened if she had stayed home instead of going out with her friends. The guilt is killing her. No matter what we say she's convinced herself this is all her fault." He sighed. "Right now she's with my parents."

Dan turned to face me. "I didn't make any brownie points with that policeman last night," he admitted, jerking his chin in Furman's direction.

"No, you didn't," I agreed. "But I understand why you were so upset. I mean, you find out your wife has been murdered and the first thing he does is start questioning you." I put a hand on his arm. "You have an alibi, Dan. There's no need to worry."

He scuffed the toe of his shoe in the grass. "No, I don't," he said. "Not really."

I stepped back, shocked and a little afraid. "You were at your sister's."

He watched the police team. "I left the cookout. I went to the park. I thought maybe I'd find Lexie and we could watch the fireworks together."

"Did you find her?"

"No. I went back to my sister's house and watched the fireworks from there." He gestured in the detective's direction. "If he doesn't know that now, he will soon enough. My sister loves me but there's no way she'd lie to the police for me. In any event, I wouldn't allow it." He turned his gaze back and looked directly into my eyes. "I was gone long enough to have been able to kill Liz and get back to my sister's house when I did. But I didn't. I

swear to you, Jackie, I didn't."
"I heard you were very angry with Liz," I said, realizing that I had backed away from Dan.
"Why wouldn't I be?" He barked a laugh. "She was trying to destroy my relationship with Lexie. Liz did everything she could to tear us apart.
"And financially? She wanted it all. She wanted me to give her the house and pay the mortgage; she wanted all of our joint account as well as half of my pension and 401(k). She wanted child support and alimony on top of that." He snorted. "There's no way I could have had a secure future if she got her way. My lawyer told me she'd never get all she wanted, but just temporary support and legal bills were killing me." He studied me closely. "In spite of everything she was doing, Jackie, I'm innocent. I would never physically hurt her or any other woman. Never. I didn't put a hand on Liz. Please, you have to believe me."
I thought. I watched the police carry out their grim tasks. I remembered almost twenty years of friendship. I surveyed Dan's ravaged face.
"Does your attorney do criminal defense work?"
He shook his head. "She said she'd give me the names of some good defense lawyers."
"Call Jeremy Barber," I said.
"Wasn't he Lars' partner?"
"One of them. He handles criminal cases. They don't get any better than Jeremy."
I took a deep breath, "You may need him. Lexie may not have an alibi. You sure don't. And you're dealing with one determined cop." Furman was standing with his hands on his hips, listening to a uniformed officer. He looked very unhappy. His partner, who looked no happier than Riley, turned her head to stare at Dan.
"I'll call today." Dan sounded relieved.
His phone rang. "I need to take this," he said after looking at the number. He stepped a few paces away. As he greeted the caller his expression softened.
I didn't mean to eavesdrop. No, that's a lie. I certainly did. I sidled

a little closer, pretending to concentrate on the activity next door. I think I leaned toward Dan so I could catch every word of his conversation. I admit it, of course I leaned. My right foot became mired in soft soil near the tree under which we were standing. My left foot barely touched the ground. I tried to remain unobtrusive as I casually rested my hand on the tree, hoping I wouldn't tilt any further.

"I'm hanging in there," Dan said in response to the caller. "This weekend? Of course, I can't – You canceled the reservation? Thank you so much. You're wonderful. I hadn't even thought of it." Now, that was interesting.

"The conference? I'm still going. Remember I have to make a presentation and if it goes well, it could be that promotion I've been talking about. The conference is after the funeral, so going shouldn't be a problem." He listened a moment. "She'll stay with my parents." More listening. "Bring her? That's a terrible idea. It's much too soon."

My antennae pricked up. This sure didn't sound like a business call.

"Come down?" Dan sounded alarmed. "No. No, wait for the conference." He listened a moment. "I'll see you then. I'll call you when I can." More noise on the other end of the phone. "You too." He disconnected and I moved (unsuspiciously I hoped) further away.

"Business colleague," he said.

"Oh," I said. Seriously? Either he didn't know how much I'd heard or he was trying to pull one over on me.

Thunder rumbled in the distance. The police seemed to be wrapping up their investigation, some cars pulling away.

"Are you going to bring Lexie back here to live when this is all behind you?" I asked.

Dan turned on me. "I don't know, Jackie. Would you like to give me your opinion? Everyone else has."

I stepped backwards. He reached out and I jumped back. His mood swings were beginning to scare me.

Dan held up his hands. "I'm sorry. It's just..." He swiped his hands across his eyes They were damp.

"Is there anything I can do?" I asked.

"Find out what happened."

"But...That's the job of the police," I protested, thinking back to my contacts with Riley Furman.

Dan's voice intensified. "You hear things. You see things."

I remembered my conversations with Bernice and Linda, as well as Nick's various revelations at this morning's interview. I had decided I was the least observant person I knew. "I really don't. I'm sort of out of the loop."

He shook his head. "You and your friends know more than you think you do. You're always looking out for each other. You're constantly talking. Just think about it."

I tried to do just that. After listening to Dan's phone conversation and the being part of the interviews with Riley my head felt like it was about to explode.

Dan looked back at the house. "How can things have gone so wrong? I loved Liz for a long time. The girl I married was so sweet and smart. We were sure we'd do great things together. And for a long time, we did. Twenty-two years...that's a long time to have everything fall apart."

"And now?"

He shook his head again. "The woman who died in that house was a stranger to me." He jerked his thumb at the jaunty sports car sitting forlornly in the driveway. "Do you know she paid cash for that thing? Where did she get the money? It wasn't from me. She may have used some of the support money I gave her, but that wasn't nearly enough. She must have squirreled money away, but where did it come from? What was she up to?" He stared at me pleadingly. "I have to know, Jackie, I have to." He looked back at the car. "Hell, if you figure this out you can have the damned car."

No, no, no. A thousand times no. Was he nuts? Bad question. Given his highs and lows in such a short period of time, I wouldn't swear to an answer right now. But to make such an offer? It felt like a bribe, although I had nothing worth buying and nothing to hide. I'd love a red sports car, but not that one. No, no, no. Although maybe if he'd accept a low offer...Stop it. No. No red BMW for me. Ever. Especially not this one.

The last police car other than Riley Furman's unmarked one left. He and his partner started toward the detective's car. She stopped and seemed to study me. I could have sworn she smiled before she turned back to the car. More importantly, I was certain, well, almost certain, at least kind of certain, that Riley wagged his fingers at me behind his back.

I pondered Dan's request. He sounded like a grieving widower. Or was he a two-timing husband? Could he be both? Or was he a cold-blooded murderer?

I sure wanted to know.

And what about Lexie? She was guilt ridden about her mother's death. That was normal, I supposed. But did she have something to feel guilty about? Right now her alibi was questionable. I couldn't bear the thought that the sweet teenager, our little Orphan Annie clone, could be anything but innocent. That would truly break my heart. I couldn't believe it. I wouldn't believe it. I had to help Lexie. Whatever way the chips fell for Dan, so be it.

The sky opened up and the rain poured down, huge drops that immediately saturated my clothes and stung with their ferocity. I turned and ran for the safety of home.

CHAPTER NINE

Watching the evening news somehow turned into a group event.

"Do you think those boobs are real?" asked Linda, peering at the screen.

"I'm sure she's had her teeth capped," said Bernice.

"Well, she certainly isn't a natural blonde," sniffed Marcia, whose hair resembled a wad of pink bubblegum.

We turned as one and stared at her. "Just saying." She popped a piece of cheese into her mouth.

"Shhh!" Bernice made a chopping movement with her hand. "Here it comes!"

A photo of Liz appeared, accompanied by a smaller picture of Dan. A video of their home played in the background. "At least they didn't show a picture of Lexie," Linda whispered.

The commentary didn't tell us anything new. The scene changed to outside of the police station.

"There's that hunky detective!" Linda said, leaning closer. A stone-faced Riley Furman pushed his way past a bank of microphones.

"Wait a minute! Who's that guy with the gray hair?" Bernice pointed toward a man with coiffed hair clad in an expensive looking suit. "That's the man we saw Liz with."

"I don't know, but that's not an off-the-rack suit he's wearing." Marcia said.

Linda sat up straighter. "Hey, I know him. He's a lawyer. He helped the hospital with some zoning work. He did a good job. Now what's his name?" She closed her eyes, flipping through her mental rolodex. Anthony? Andy? No, that's not right. Aaron. Aaron Winters. His wife is a pharmaceutical representative. Real

go getter." She thought some more. "Patty. Patty Winters. Their daughter graduated from St. Agnes last year." She opened her eyes and smiled triumphantly.
"Wife, huh?" Bernice said. "He sure didn't look married the way he was behaving at that dinner."
"While the cat's away..." I offered.
Linda nodded. "Patty travels a lot for her job. That cat's away a lot. And with their daughter at college..."
We shared a significant look.
"Why should we worry about it?" Marcia replied. "He's at the police station. Maybe he's already being questioned."
"And maybe it's a coincidence," Linda said.
I heard the detective's remarks about amateurs replay in my head. "I think we call Detective Furman, tell him what we know and leave it at that."
"That's it?" Bernice raised one eyebrow. "Don't you want to know more about his relationship with Liz? I think we should find out the truth before we talk to the police."
I tugged my hair. "No! It's none of our business." I felt my resolve waiver, however, as I remembered my encounter with Dan. Boy, did I have something to tell the girls.
"It's for Lexie," Marcia said softly. "And for Dan, too. Do you really think the police care about the whole story?"
"Yes," I said, picturing Riley Furman's serious gray eyes.
My friends were silent. Bernice examined her fingernails. Linda sat with her arms crossed, her foot tapping. Marcia had assumed the lotus position and tilted her head upward, doing some weird breathing exercises.
'For Lexie,' I thought.
"We need to find out who killed Liz and why," Bernice said. "Our friends are in trouble."
I was silent for a moment. Dan had asked us to help, hadn't he? I decided to unload on my friends, and it was going to be a heavy load. I went to the fridge and pulled out another bottle of wine.
"I have a lot to tell you," I said. They looked at me expectantly.
"Let me start with the worst part first. Lexie may not have an

alibi for the time of her mother's murder."

"What?" Linda's hand slipped and she almost dropped the wine she was pouring into our glasses. "I thought she was with Nick and Max."

I shook my head. "Apparently she went off with some girls from the tennis team."

"Well, that isn't so bad," Marcia said soothingly. "All we have to do is ask Lexie who they were and get them to tell the police she was with them."

My shoulders relaxed a bit. "You're right. I'm making a big deal out of this. It will probably be very easy to do that and then she'll be off the hook."

We all smiled.

"Unless someone murdered Liz for her," Bernice said ominously.

"For Heaven's sake!" Linda snapped. "Are you reading thrillers again? This isn't Strangers on a Train, you know."

Bernice nodded. "You're right. But Max told the police he saw those girls without Lexie that evening."

Crap!

"She probably just went to the bathroom," Marcia said, but she looked worried.

"Speaking of Max," I said, leaning toward Bernice, "Do you know he has a girlfriend?"

"I found out during the interview," Bernice said. "He's in love with Julie, his chemistry partner." She laughed. "I didn't know whether to strangle him for not telling me or say it was about time. Frankly, I'd gotten a little suspicious. Most boys don't take half an hour getting ready for school." We all laughed with her. "Nick has a girlfriend, too, you know. Or at least he likes a girl."

"It's amazing what will come out at a police interview," I said wryly. "He won't tell me who it is. Do you know?"

"Max finally spilled the beans. Her name is Kelly.

She's Vietnamese-American, incredibly cute and captain of the debate team."

"Well, he certainly could do worse," I said.

"Ladies, welcome to the next phase of parenthood," Marcia said,

raising her glass. "I'm sure Bill won't be far behind."
"OK," Linda said, getting us back on track," Lexie probably has an alibi but we need to find out who she was with every minute between leaving her house and returning after the fireworks. I bet the boys could help us with this. There may not be many gaps to fill in. In fact, there may not be any."
"I'm not sure I want Bill involved," Marcia frowned. "He's upset enough as it is, and if I ask him to check up on Lexie he could get really scared."
"Nick already is," I said. "He asked Detective Furman if Lexie is a suspect and the detective didn't beat around the bush. She is."
Linda groaned and took a gulp of wine.
I loaded a chip with humus. "We need a plan. Let me talk to Nick about needing to verify Lexie's alibi. He already knows the police have her on their short list of suspects and he's probably the closest to her of the three boys. I'll tackle him this evening."
Bernice nodded. "Good idea. We can talk to the other boys if Nick and Lexie can't fill in the entire time frame."
"What's next?" Marcia asked. "You said you have a lot to tell us."
"Dan definitely doesn't have an alibi."
There was a collective gasp.
"How can that be?" Bernice asked, frowning. "I very clearly heard him tell the policeman he was at his sister's house."
"It turns out he went to the park looking for Lexie," I replied. "He confessed he was gone long enough to have driven to the house, killed Liz, and returned to his sister's place."
"Did he see Lexie?" Bernice asked.
"He says not."
"If I were a mystery novelist the two of them would be in it together," Bernice said.
My friends looked at me expectantly. "Yes," I said slowly, "that would be a good plot twist. But I can't believe it. Not of Lexie."
"What about Dan?" Marcia asked.
"Normally I'd say no, but he was pretty volatile today. He scared me a couple times."
"Is there anything else you'd like to tell us?" Linda asked a bit sar-

castically. "I'm already feeling pretty overwhelmed."

"I think Dan's having an affair." They all gaped at me.

"Why in the world do you think that?" Marcia asked.

I told them about the conversation on which I had eavesdropped. "From the tone of his voice and what I overheard, that wasn't a business conversation."

"What does it matter?" Bernice asked. "He and Liz have been separated for several months. There's nothing to say he can't have a relationship with another woman. Liz certainly doesn't seem to have let being married stop her."

"You're right," I said, "But let's think about this a little more. Dan told Ray Liz was bleeding him dry, right?" They all nodded. "He told me the same thing. Take it one step further. Dan wants a future with this new woman, but he's afraid of not having enough money for himself, never mind someone else."

Marcia nodded thoughtfully. "If Liz were out of the way that wouldn't be a problem. He'd have everything; a new woman, his relationship with Lexie, plenty of money."

"Dan asked us to help him," I said.

We were all silent for a while, sipping our wine and avoiding each other's eyes.

"Seems to me," Linda finally said, "Dan's got himself into a bit of a pickle. I don't know how to deal with him. On top of that, Lexie's still my top priority."

We all agreed.

"I think we need to know what Dan's been up to." Marcia finally piped up. "Why don't we simply ask him if he has a girlfriend?"

"Do you really think he'd tell us the truth?" Bernice asked.

"I don't know." Marcia admitted.

"If we ask him and he doesn't tell us, or he lies, we've warned him we suspect something. He could break it off, he could delete any calls or texts, he could get her to disappear from his life for a while." Linda said. "I vote we find out some other way."

"I vote we let Riley Furman find out," I said.

"Vote!" Marcia said. "Everyone in favor of finding out if Dan Williams has a girlfriend raise their hand." Three hands shot into

the air.
"Well?" Marcia challenged me.
I hesitated.
"Majority rules," she declared.
Since when? Were we turning into some kind of girl detective club? Where was a copy of Roberts' Rules of Order when you needed it?
"Now that we've decided," Bernice said, "How are we going to do this?"
"Simple," Marcia said. "We follow him."
"Now, wait a minute," I protested. "What are we going to do, put on trench coats and dark glasses and hide behind bushes? Happen to coincidentally be on the same plane the next time he leaves on a business trip? Or maybe we should tail him on the highway if he's driving to his appointments." I held my hands out, palms up. "Ladies, this is crazy. We don't have the slightest idea what we're doing."
"You have a legitimate point," Linda said. "However, it doesn't mean we don't investigate. How hard can it be? I'm willing to bet this girlfriend isn't a local. All we need to do is get his schedule for when he's going out of town next, and *then* we follow him." She smiled triumphantly.
I moaned and put my head in my hands.
"So, what about this Aaron Winters character?" Marcia asked.
I moaned again.
"What about him?" Bernice asked.
"We need to find out what was going on between him and Liz."
"Do you have a suggestion?" I asked worriedly.
"Of course," Marcia said. "We ask him."
"Just walk up and ask him? What are you going to say? Hi, my name's Marcia. Were you having a fling with my friend Liz? Oh, and by the way, did you kill her?" I took a slug of wine.
"Sarcasm doesn't become you," Marcia said sternly.
"Maybe I could try to feel Patty out next time I see her," Linda offered.
Bernice shook her head. "Are you going to ask her if her hus-

band's having an affair? That would go over well. Great conversation opener. And I'm not sure it would work."

Linda thought a while. "I'm sure I can come up with something. I'll let you guys know."

Oh, good. I could hardly wait.

CHAPTER TEN

The door to the kitchen slammed. I turned to admonish my son, but stopped at the sight of the thunderstorm crossing his face. Max followed close behind, looking equally unhappy.

"What's up?" I asked.

"The kids in our school are jerks!" Nick threw his backpack to the floor. He opened our cookie jar and stuffed a treat into his mouth.

"It's really bad, Mrs. O," Max confirmed. "A bunch of them are saying Lexie killed her mom."

I gasped.

"A lot of them won't talk to her at all. Others laugh at her and say nasty things when she goes by." He snagged a cookie from the jar.

"The worst are these stuck-up girls she thought were her friends."

"Let me guess. Cheerleaders." I thought of the girl who had come between Lexie and her boyfriend.

Nick nodded. "Some of them. Not all. But the guys aren't much better."

"The ones who don't think Lexie did it say it was her dad." Max accepted a glass of milk.

"That's awful," I said. "What did you do when you found out what they were saying?"

"We stuck up for her," said Nick, puffing out his chest. Then his shoulders sagged. "But it wasn't easy. They started calling us a bunch of names, too."

"Some of the nerdy kids were nice," said Max. He looked surprised. Ah hah. Life lesson hopefully learned.

"Lexie was crying in study hall," Nick said. "The teacher was really nice to her. She took Lexie to see the counselor."
"Man, did the teacher let us have it when she came back. I didn't know a teacher could get so mad." Max looked surprised again. Another lesson. Teachers are human.
Nick chimed in. "She made everyone put their cell phones in a basket." Now *there* was a punishment. "Then she separated all the girls who were talking about Lexie and said they couldn't sit together for the rest of the school year." Better and better.
"Last thing, she assigned everybody an essay to write on kindness, character or the meaning of friendship."
"And it's due Monday," Max groaned. He hated writing assignments. Max's brain was wired for math and science.
"Who was the teacher?" I asked.
"Ms. Sherwood."
Ms. Sherwood was a tiny blonde who seemed so sweet. All the boys had a crush on her.
'You go, girl!' I thought. I made a mental note to do something special for her. Maybe I'd make her some fresh brownies. "How did the other kids react?" I asked.
"A lot of them clapped when she told those girls off," Nick replied. "Even some of the cool kids."
Maybe there was hope for the human race.
"No one clapped for homework," Max clarified.
That was OK. I wouldn't have clapped for homework either.
"Lexie's dad picked her up early. He had Reverend Scruggs with him," Max said. There at least was a piece of good news.
"Mom! We have to do something!" Nick finally bent down to great Maggie, who had been dancing by his feet.
"What do you want to do?"
"Show everybody Lexie didn't do it."
"How do you propose to do that?" I asked.
He and Max looked at each other. "Maybe we should write down everything we know?" He looked at me inquiringly.
"I don't know that it will be much," I said, "But let's try. Come with me."

We settled in my office, me at my desk, Max on the loveseat and Nick stretched out on the floor with Maggie beside him.

"First," I reminded Nick. "You were going to ask Lexie to give you the names of everybody she was with after the party."

"He nodded. She said Detective Furman asked her to do the same thing." So, the amateurs were on the right track. "She's working on it."

"Was she alone at any time during the evening?"

Nick shook his head. "She said that even when she went to bathroom she saw someone she knows. I think she's going to be ok."

Max chimed in. "I still can't believe that policeman said Lexie's a suspect. That's pretty lame."

"He's just doing his job," I said. "The quicker he can eliminate her, the quicker he can consider someone else."

"I don't want it to be her dad, either," Nick said.

"None of us do." I sighed. Then I thought of Marcia and Linda's outrageous scheme to follow Dan and grimaced.

"Mom, what's wrong with your face? Are you having a stroke or something?" Nick asked in alarm.

"I can call 911," Max volunteered, reaching for his phone.

I held up my hand. "I'm fine. I was just thinking about something Marcia said."

"I'll bet it was kind of strange," Nick said.

"You could say that," I muttered. "Now, where were we? What do we know?" I held my pen at the ready.

"Lexie hadn't been getting along with her mom," Max said.

"So what?" Nick asked. "A lot of kids don't."

I wrote it down anyway.

"Mrs. Williams had an expensive new car and Mr. Williams said he didn't pay for it."

I made a note of that also.

"Things had gotten weird over there," Max said.

"What exactly does that mean?"

The boys looked at each other, then down at the floor. "Ok, so here's the deal," Nick said.

I waited, pen at the ready.

"We think Mrs. Williams was dealing drugs," Max told the floor.
"WHAT?" My pen skidded across the paper.
I gathered my wits about me, or at least tried to. "What makes you think that?"
"We're talking steroids, Mom," Nick explained. "After Mr. Williams moved out, a bunch of college jocks started hanging around. You saw some of them at the party."
I nodded. "Maybe they just wanted to get to know Lexie and her friends," I said. "They're awfully cute and some guys prefer to date off campus." I remembered that from my own undergraduate days when men from my own university would drive to a local woman's college to meet girls rather than go out with us coeds. It had been very annoying, particularly as there was no corresponding men's college in the area.
"Maybe that was part of it," Max said, "but let's think about it." He held up his fingers and started to count. "Number one; how would Mrs. Williams meet these guys? Did she drive over to the campus and put up notices saying 'I have a cute daughter. Anyone who wants to go out with her call this number?'"
I bit back a smile. He had a point.
"Number two; would you bring around a bunch of girls to date Nick, even though they were years older than he was?"
No way. Another good point.
Nick took up the argument. "Do you remember I told you about seeing Mrs. Williams with the super fit guy at the park and him giving her a piece of paper?" I nodded. Frankly, I hadn't thought much of it when Nick mentioned it to me.
"That's not the only time we saw them. And we saw Mrs. Williams give some of the jocks papers that looked the same."
"I'm sure I saw one of them slip her some money when he came over to her house," Max said.
"Next number," Max said, holding up another digit. "Some of these guys are world class athletes, hoping to get into the pros. And everyone knows about steroids."
'Please don't say everyone does it,' I thought.
"Not everyone uses them," Nick said. "But think about all those

Russian athletes."

"And Lance Armstrong," contributed Max, who still mourned the downfall of his cycling idol.

"We think those papers were prescriptions," Nick said. "Maybe they were stolen. Maybe they were forged. One of my friends knows the guy from the park. He says he's a personal trainer at the gym Mrs. Williams went to. Can't they get their hands on prescriptions?"

"Not legally," I said. "I suppose there are unethical doctors they could get them from. Or maybe some doctors are really careless and leave prescription pads where someone could steal them." I felt like my world was falling apart. "How would Liz even know about steroids? And why would she even get involved in something like this?"

"You can get a lot of money from selling steroids," Nick said. "Maybe the trainer was selling to one or two people, and then he and Liz decided it wouldn't be so suspicious if she was actually handling the money. They teamed up and she sold to a lot more."

I blanched. How could two sixteen-year-olds be so savvy? This conversation frightened me more for our children than any other I could recall.

"Do you think all those young men were using steroids?" I asked.

"We don't know," Nick admitted.

"I don't think Teddy is," Max said. "You remember him. He's going out with Anna."

I recalled seeing him at the party and at the library when interviews were taking place. "He seems like a real straight shooter. He was the only one of those guys who decided Lexie was too young for him. After all, he's a college sophomore and she's only going to be a high school junior. He told her they could only be friends."

"What did Lexie think of that?" I asked, aware we were venturing away from the subject.

"She was happy," Nick said. "Some of those other guys hit on her pretty hard."

I knew this already and found that, the more that I thought

about Liz setting up those blind dates, the angrier I got. And now to think some of them might have been buying drugs from Liz? The situation was intolerable. I had a dreadful thought. What if Dan had found out? What would he do to protect his little girl?

"Mom," Nick said. "What do we do now?"

"Do?" I repeated. "What do we do about what?"

"About the drugs," Nick said with exaggerated patience. "Do we call that detective?"

"And tell him what?" I asked "That you think your neighbor sold drugs? Did you ever see any drugs? Did you hear anyone talking about it? Did you actually see a prescription?"

The boys shook their heads. They had been animated discussing their theory but now they looked dejected, with slumped shoulders and downturned mouths. Obviously, I had burst their bubble. "I think you need to have some evidence before you go to the police," I said. I tried to soften my message. "I could be wrong, though. Tell you what. I'll call Attorney Barber and see what he thinks. How does that sound?"

"Teddy works part time at the gym," Max offered. "Maybe you could talk to him."

"That's a possibility," I replied. "Let me think a while and talk to the lawyer." I smiled at them. "I am really proud of you for telling me all this. It must have been hard." They nodded. "Let's take a break and we'll talk again later, ok?"

They agreed.

"Why don't you take Maggie to the park? She's waited for you all day." Maggie gave Nick her patented snaggletooth smile.

The boys rose and shuffled out of the room. I watched them leave. As soon as I was sure they were gone I called Jeremy Barber.

"Hi, Jeremy, do you have a minute?"

"For you, always," he replied. "What can I do for you?"

"Did Dan Williams call you?" I asked.

"He did. We scheduled an appointment for this evening. Thank for the referral."

"You're welcome. I have an important question."

"Shoot."

"If you suspect something about a murder suspect but don't have proof, should you tell the police your suspicions?"

"Jackie, you'd better spell out what you're talking about."

I outlined my conversation with the boys. Jeremy was quiet for such a long time I thought we had been disconnected. "Well," he said finally, "That's a very interesting question. If the boys had proof, I'd say they absolutely should let the police know. The drugs might not be connected to the murder, but it would be up to the detectives to figure that out." He paused. "When you suspect something, it's not so clear. If you say nothing, there's an argument that you're obstructing an investigation." My heart dropped. "But I don't think it's a very strong one. You have to remember also that there are laws about libel and slander, so you have to be careful what you say." Yea! There was a reason to do nothing. "However, they normally wouldn't apply in this situation." I had forgotten what it felt like to deal with a lawyer. Couldn't they ever just say what they meant? "Bottom line is, I don't think currently the boys have a duty to tell the police what they think. But if I were a detective, I'd certainly want to hear it."

'Well, thanks for nothing,' I thought. 'That was as clear as mud.'

"Jackie," Jeremy said, his voice stern, "If I accept Dan Williams as a client, I'll need to be very careful about conflicts of interest. Is there anything that could implicate you or Nick in the Williams murder?"

"No. Nothing. We'd like to help Dan and Lexie if we can. That's all that's going on."

"Well good," Jeremy said. "Because if there is even the slightest doubt in your mind I won't take his case. You and Nick will always come first."

My heart swelled with love for this wonderful friend. "Thank you, Jeremy," I said. "I love you too."

He cleared his throat. "I see you and Mary have that dinner on the calendar. I'll see you then." He hung up.

I picked up the phone again. Time for another meeting of the girl detective club. I could only imagine what my friends were going to say.

CHAPTER ELEVEN

Bernice scrunched up her beautiful face. "What was the name the boys told you?"

"Adam. Adam Wright."

She closed her eyes. "There are several trainers at the gym. What did he look like again?"

"Sandy hair. A little under six feet. Of course, a great build."

"That goes without saying." Bernice kept her eyes closed. "Let me think."

"Do you have a trainer?" Marcia asked.

"His name is Ray," Bernice replied without opening her eyes. Of course she was referring to her husband. "He's a sadist."

"What about you?" Marcia asked Linda.

"Nope. Too much work. And you?"

"Yes, but it's a she, not a he."

No one bothered to ask me. I didn't belong to the gym, nor did I want to. My slogan of everything in moderation applied to exercise, not just unhealthy things like alcohol and chocolate.

Bernice's eyes flew open. "Oh yes, I know who he is. He works with several women I know. They sing his praises."

"What about Liz?" I asked.

"She didn't seem to stick with any trainer in particular. I think she had her routine pretty well figured out. Now that I think about it, though, I did notice her talking to him several times. One or two times it seemed pretty intense. I kept my distance because I figured it wasn't any of my business."

"So now we know who Andy Wright is," said Linda, "What do we do about it?"

"We go to the gym and check him out." Bernice smiled.

"I like the boys' idea of talking to Teddy first," I said. "I understand he works part time at the gym."

Marcia nodded. "I've seen him there quite a bit. He seems to get stuck serving at the juice bar a lot." She looked at me speculatively. "We could take you in with a guest pass," she said. "That would give you an excuse to look around." Her eyes narrowed and she squinted at me. "But first we go shopping," she announced.

"Why would we do that?" I asked.

"You're crazy if you think you're going to wear one of your ratty T-shirts to the gym. It simply isn't done."

Leave it to my friends to belong to a high fashion gym.

Let me state unequivocally that I hate spandex. It squeezes you in some places so that you can't breathe and squeezes you out in others like a ruptured disc. In recent years we have been tortured by the sight of heavy set, nay, obese women stuffing their bodies into what appear to be sausage casings and prancing around like they're Miss Universe contestants. Everything wiggles and jiggles and pops out so that they more resemble the Pillsbury dough boy than a beauty queen. It is not a good look, and someone has to put a stop to it. I am doing my very small part by refusing to wear the stuff. Moreover, what about men in their stretchy shorts and no jock straps? Ewww. Too much information there, guys.

There are only certain, very trim body types that look good in spandex. Of course, all my friends qualified. Well, the old saying is that there's one in every crowd who's different. Yep, that was me. No spandex. End of subject.

Before I knew it, I was standing in a high-end athletic clothing store surveying myself in the mirror. My friends kept pulling outfits off the racks for me to try on. I kept trying to put them back. Ultimately, I was unsuccessful and here I stood wearing spandex leggings and a sports top that cut off at my midriff. I surveyed myself critically in the mirror. It could have been worse, but if anyone seemed to need a trainer, I supposed I looked the part. I looked around and spotted a display of gym shorts and coordinated shirts. That was more my style! As I moved toward it Marcia grabbed my elbow and steered me back to the mirror. "Do you know how it looks if you do leg lifts in gym shorts?" She had a point. But I wasn't going to do any leg lifts, was I? In fact, I wasn't intending to do any exercise at all.

"I think you look cute," Bernice said. "And look, here's a matching headband."

I took the headband and eased it over my forehead. I did like the headband. And I liked the color of the outfit, a nice mix of turquoise and blue. Once again I veered off into the T-shirt section. Ah hah! I spotted some tunic like tops that coordinated with my outfit. I grabbed one and pulled it over my head. I pirouetted, watching my reflection. Actually, I didn't look bad at all.

"Get that," Linda said encouragingly. "You can wear that and the leggings on a date."

What date? I hadn't been on a date in years. I had no intention of going on a date in the near future. The clothing was surprisingly comfortable, however, and this would be a great outfit to wear at the grocery store, or walking the dog, or just to hang out at home. I closed my eyes for a second. I couldn't believe it. I was going to buy spandex. What about my protest agenda? Well, I was the only one who had the slightest idea I was waging a one-woman protest. Maybe this was like losing a skirmish but not the war.

"Look! They have it in pink." Bernice dangled another outfit in front of me. Ooh! That was cute. I snatched it from her and headed to the fitting room.

"Now for the shoes," Marcia said after I had handed my selections to the saleswoman.

"What's wrong with my Nikes?" I asked. "I'm only walking into the gym once, after all. I have no intention of joining."

"Those are walking shoes. You need a more all around pair of shoes."

"Why? Walking is what I do for exercise. And some biking. And maybe swimming, but I don't wear shoes in the pool."

Linda held up a pair of white shoes with turquoise stripes and pink and turquoise laces. "These are on sale," she said, "And they go with everything you're buying. Plus, they're a good quality workout shoe."

Oh dear. How could $100 possibly be a sale price?

By the time we left the store my credit card was smoking. Maybe my book advance was going to pay for sports clothes rather than a car for Nick. I resolved not to tell him.

"All right, ladies!" Marcia clapped her hands. "We're ready. Let's go home and all get changed and then beard the lion in his den."

I couldn't say I liked that analogy. Somehow I didn't think facing a lion in a den would have a happy ending. Just think of the poor gladiators.

Half an hour later we were in Bernice's SUV heading out to talk to Teddy and Adam Wright. "Shouldn't we walk?" I asked. "It isn't far."

"Why would we do that?" Linda asked.

"It seems silly to drive to a gym to exercise when we could exercise getting there."

"It's too humid out. It would ruin my hair if we walked," Marcia said. She had coaxed her head into a curly, almost frizzy, style with enough styling gel to look like she had just come out of the shower. Seriously? There was no way humidity was affecting that helmet.

I felt Linda shaking with laughter beside me. "I give up," I muttered.

To say that the gym was state of the art was an understatement. It was a glowing silver structure with a peaked metal roof that gleamed strongly in the sunlight. It hurt to look at it without sunglasses. The name of the gym was emblazoned across the front in opalescent letters that threatened to blind anyone looking at them. I squinted at them. The letters were so stylistically done that I couldn't have told you the gym's name if I didn't already know it. That didn't seem like a particularly good marketing plan to me. Inside was an expansive entry with a chrome and marble check-in desk manned by a pert teenager with a perfect spandexed body and a gigantic smile. "Hello, welcome!" she chirped. "Are you checking in?"

"We are." My friends presented identification cards. "We have a guest pass for our friend here. She's thinking of joining."
"How wonderful!" She clapped her hands. I'd be willing to bet she was a cheerleader. "Would you like a tour?" She whipped her head around. "I think Tammy's available. She can show you all of our equipment. We have a sauna and a wonderful spa I'm sure you'd love."
"Thanks anyway," Linda said. "We'll show her around."
The cheerleader seemed to deflate slightly. She appeared to remember she was meant to be upbeat and gave us another toothy smile. "Just let us know if you need anything. Have fun."
"Too much energy," Bernice muttered. "It wears me out just talking to her."
We pushed through the double doors behind the reception desk. To either side were signs for locker rooms and restrooms. Ahead of us was an array of machines that seemed to stretch for miles. There were rowing machines, running machines, machines for all different types of muscle exercises and rows and rows of weights. I had to admit it was impressive. Unlike many gyms, it smelled slightly spicy rather than sweaty. I wondered what they used for air freshener. I could use some of that at home, particularly when Maggie had been busy rubbing her scent all over the couch – and the rug, and the bed, and whatever else she could think of.
"The indoor pool is to the right," Linda told me gesturing. "We have swimming teams, along with water aerobics classes. To the left is the indoor jogging track. There's an outside track out back. The spa is just beyond the pool. You can get wonderful body treatments there and they just started doing nails." She was as good a guide as Tammy ever would have been. I suspected she was hoping I'd join so I could take advantage of my new spandex.
"Nice," I admitted, surveying the large room. The people working out seemed to be very focused on their exercises. There was a lot of spandex on the types of bodies that looked good wearing it.
"It seems awfully competitive," I said, watching a group of bodybuilders work out with weights.

"I never thought of it that way," Marcia said, looking around with me. "But I guess it is."

"I think the Y is more my speed," I said. She sighed.

"That's Adam Wright," Bernice said out of the corner of her mouth, using her chin to indicate a well muscled man spotting a woman working with free weights. He was a good looking young man, apparently a body builder himself. Muscles rippled under his stretchy shirt and when he demonstrated a technique with weights the veins popped out on his arm. I noticed several women watching him appreciatively. He wasn't my type. I prefer a leaner, if well toned body, and his facial features were a little too perfect for my taste. I could certainly understand how women would be attracted to him, however. He helped the woman rise to her feet off the workbench. In my mind his hand lingered on her just a fraction too long, but if it did, she didn't seem to notice. Either that or she liked it.

"The juice bar is over here," Linda said, breaking my concentration. "It's just through those doors."

"Are we sure Teddy's there?" I asked.

"No," she replied, "but I usually see him at the bar in the afternoon. Keep your fingers crossed he's there today."

We entered an open, sunlit room. Around it chairs and tables were arranged in groupings that invited conversation. The chairs were made of silver metal and sported cushioned seats and backs of dark teal and magenta. Modern art on the walls picked up those colors and added splashes of yellow and orange. On the wall to the right was a bar with several stools. Behind the bar were bottles of fruit juices and bins overflowing with fruits such as bananas and strawberries and vegetables like kale and spinach.

"They make a really good kale mango smoothie," Marcia offered. Yuck!

"I like the blueberry pomegranate," Bernice volunteered.

That sounded better.

"Raspberry for me," said Linda.

I could do raspberry. "I suppose they don't have chocolate," I said.

My friends just stared at me and Marcia shook her head as if I were pathetic.

Teddy was behind the bar washing a blender. We greeted him and placed our orders. I decided on a strawberry banana smoothie. That actually sounded good.

Teddy placed our orders on the bar.

"So," Marcia said, "What do you know about steroids?"

Bernice choked and spit her drink back into her glass.

Linda sighed and pounded her head on the bar's surface.

There was nothing subtle about good old Marcia.

Teddy stared at her like a deer in headlights.

"Let's start over," I said. Poor Teddy was shifting his eyes from side to side, looking for an escape. "We're trying to help Lexie and her dad. We heard rumors that Mrs. Williams was selling steroids, probably to kids at your school, and that they were coming from this gym. If that's true it might mean someone other than her family had reason to kill her. The police seem to be focused on Lexie and her father and we want to do what we can to get them out of the spotlight. We didn't want to lead the police on a wild goose chase, so we thought we'd ask what you know."

"I don't do steroids," Teddy said, his mouth said in a grim line. "And shouldn't the cops be asking these questions anyway?"

"That can be arranged," Marcia said, reaching for her phone.

Teddy blanched. "I don't know anything for sure. If I tell you what I've heard, or what I think will you leave me alone?"

I shook my head. "We can't promise that."

He hesitated. Marcia fingered her phone.

"I'm on a baseball scholarship at the college," Teddy said. "It's the only way I can afford to go there."

"Teddy," Bernice said gently, "We have no interest in getting you in trouble. If you do lead us to something concrete, we'll tell Detective Furman, who is leading the investigation. He won't be out to get you, I'm sure. He wants to find out who killed Mrs. Williams just like we do. If you don't hide facts from him or lie to him, you'll be fine. And if you truly don't know anything, this conversation stops here."

Teddy polished the bar with a towel. "Like I said, I'm on scholarship." He finally looked at us directly. "I'm one of seven children. My parents help as much as they can, but they can't afford to send any of us to college. I'm the first one in my family to get past high school. If I used steroids and they found out it would break their hearts. So there's no way I'm going to get near any drugs."

"That's good," Linda said sympathetically. "I don't think all of the athletes at your school feel the same."

He shook his head. "They don't. Some of them want to get into the pros so bad they look for any edge they can find, and sometimes it means they take steroids. I think they're stupid. The coaches test randomly and if you're caught, you're off the team. If you're on scholarship that's taken away. It's a huge risk." He threw his towel into the laundry behind the counter. "A lot of these guys don't care about getting an education. They just want to go professional. And you know what happens half the time? They go pro before they graduate and then they get cut or they get injured and can't play." He pointed a finger at his chest. "*I'm* going to graduate. If I don't make the pros, I'm going to grad school to be an architect. I'm going to make my parents proud. And I'm going to be someone my brothers and sisters look up to. If I can I'm going to help them get through school. Steroids? Not me."

My vision felt blurry. What a peach. If I had a daughter I'd want her to find someone like Teddy.

Marcia smiled and put her hand gently on top of his. "That's so commendable. If I could think of a way to help you I would. But now we need to focus on the question at hand. Do you know if Mrs. Williams was selling steroids?"

"I don't know for sure," he said. "Several of the guys you saw at her party talked about her a lot and said she was really friendly. A couple times one or two of them came back from her house with what looked like prescriptions. I didn't get close enough to know what they were for sure, but I think they were for steroids because the guys always seemed pumped up and excited, like they had won a big game."

"Do you think she could have been working with someone at the gym?"

Teddy frowned. "There are always steroids floating around the gym. Some of the members use them and I'd be willing to bet some of them sell them. I'd say the body builders are most likely to use, but these days every sport has people who do. The managers keep an eye out for that kind of stuff. If they see anyone using, they'll expel them from the gym. They always say if they catch anyone selling, they'll call the cops, but it hasn't happened since I've been here."

"Do you think any of the personal trainers could be selling?"

Teddy thought. "It's possible. Not that I know of though."

"What do you know about Adam Wright?" I asked.

"Adam?" He wrinkled his nose. "He's a good trainer. Knows what he's doing. I think he makes pretty good money. From the trainers I know, he'd be the one I'd pick to do something like this. He has expensive tastes, drives a fancy car, and likes to wear gold chains and a big flashy watch when he's not working. He's cocky, too. He thinks he's a real lady's man. And he works with a lot of body builders. Yeah, if I had to choose someone, he'd be the one." He surveyed us. "But I don't know for sure. Don't go telling that detective otherwise. I'm just guessing."

"Don't worry, Teddy," Linda said, draining her smoothie. "We're just guessing too. Our friends are in a bad spot and if we can find anything that makes the police look for more suspects, that's what we need to do."

Teddy nodded. "I respect that." A group of women pushed open the doors to the juice bar and headed in Teddy's direction.

"What now, my friends?" Bernice asked.

"Now we do that lion and the den thing." I replied.

CHAPTER TWELVE

With coaxing from the ladies I started out my exercise by using a treadmill. That wasn't so bad. I could do this. Of course, I was walking and Bernice was flying on the machine next to me. Linda was doing weights and I had no idea what Marcia was doing, but she seemed to be imitating a pretzel.

Adam Wright walked up to me and I explained that I was visiting and trying to decide whether to join the gym. He asked me about my goals and I made them up. He took me to a weight machine and I started an exercise that was challenging, but not over the top. He stood by, giving me encouragement and tips on how to use the equipment safely.

"I think you worked with my friend Liz Williams," I said, starting to breathe heavily.

"Sometimes," he admitted.

Bernice approached doing something that looked absurdly difficult with a set of dumbbells. "You've worked with several women I know," she said.

"I have a lot of clients," Adam replied.

"I'll bet you know a lot of moves," Linda cooed, stepping closer and toweling off her décolletage.

He flashed her a crooked smile. "You could say so." He stepped over to Marcia and slipped his hands along her back as she stepped off the machine she had been using. He smiled directly at her and she swatted at him. "Hands!" Something like a growl came from the back of Marcia's throat. Adam looked alarmed.

He stepped back, still smiling, holding his hands up. "Just trying to help."

"You knew Liz pretty well, didn't you?" Linda asked continuing to remove sweat from her upper body.

"Well, yeah."

"And you work with a lot of college athletes," Bernice contributed. "I've heard them talk about you." Liar, liar pants on fire. "I teach at the university," she said as if that explained her knowing the athletes. I doubted many, if any of them, were in her theoretical math classes.

Marcia, Bernice and Linda were now all using their towels to some effect. Adam was watching them with widening eyes. If this continued our corner of the gym would look as though we were rehearsing a scene for a grade B college movie. A really, really bad grade B movie. I used my towel to wipe sweat off my face. It wasn't sexy, but the moisture was definitely disturbing my vision.

"I don't know a lot of college kids," Adam said to Bernice. "Most of them work out on campus."

"But Liz knew them, didn't she?" Marcia stopped her gyrations and took a step closer. "You two were in business together, weren't you?"

"I don't know what you're talking about," Adam protested, trying to back away.

Linda gasped. "I know what you were doing!" she exclaimed. I hope she did, because I was still at sea. "Liz would set athletes up on dates with her daughter. Then she would sound them out about steroids. If they were interested, you'd give her a prescription and the two of you would share the profits." Eureka! That's how it worked. "Where did you get the prescriptions? Do you have a doctor friend who doesn't mind making a little extra on the side?"

Adam had turned pale. His eyes were darting from side to side frantically as he looked for an escape route. "You're crazy," he hissed. "And if you tell anyone I'm selling steroids I'll sue you for everything you're worth."

"Truth is an absolute defense," I said, repeating something Lars had said in connection with one of the firm's cases.

Adam tried to turn away but was stopped by a woman in leopard tights who walked by and stroked his arm. "So much fun, darling," she said. "Let's do it again soon." He acknowledged her with a faint smile. A grey-haired tigress in purple gave him a hug on her way to the weight machines.

A young red head walked over and slapped his face. Everyone in the gym stopped what they were doing and turned to stare. "How could you!" she whispered, tears running down her cheeks. "I thought I could trust you. Why are you trying to ruin me? You and Liz Williams were trying to break up my marriage."

"I don't know what you're talking about," Adam protested.

"You liar," she hissed. "I can't take anymore."

"Lisa." Adam reached out toward her.

"Don't touch me," she said. "Don't you dare touch me ever again." She ran toward the changing room.

"Don't worry, sweetie," said another woman, swatting Adam with a towel. "There are plenty more where she came from."

I heard that growling noise again. Bernice surreptitiously kicked Marcia's ankle.

Linda looked around the room at several smiling women. "Oh, my God!" she said. "Are you having affairs with all these women?"

Adam blanched and started to walk backwards.

"Liz knew," I said. "Was she blackmailing you?" I thought Adam was going to faint. Suddenly the truth registered. "She wasn't blackmailing you," I said, "Well, maybe she was. But the real money was in blackmailing the women you were sleeping with, wasn't it? What did you do? Split the proceeds, just like with the steroids? Quite an enterprise the two of you had going."

"It's time for my break." Adam turned and literally ran from the room. Once again, the room went still, the clack of equipment silenced. Several pairs of eyes stared at us.

"What have we stumbled into?" Bernice asked.

Slowly, casually, we made our way toward the exit.

"Proof," Linda whispered. "We need proof. How are we going to get it?"

"Ask," Marcia replied. "Get the name of that redhead. Seems like a good place to start."

I opened my mouth to speak. "Don't you dare tell us to talk to Riley Furman," Marcia said.

"I think that woman's proof enough." I protested.

Bernice dropped her towel into a laundry bin. "I'm beginning to think you're right."

Marcia wheeled around. "Vote!" she commanded. "Everyone in favor of talking to her first raise your hand." She surveyed us sternly. "What if we're wrong? Do you want to cause trouble by sending the police after her? What would that do to her marriage if her husband found out?" She stomped her foot. "Vote!"

"What was the question again?" Bernice asked, stalling for time.

"All in favor of talking to her first, raise your hand," Marcia raised her hand. Linda fist pumped the air. Bernice hesitated and then raised her hand.

"She has a point," She told me.

I sighed and raised my hand halfway.

"What is that supposed to mean?" Marcia demanded.

"All for one and one for all," I replied throwing my towel in the container. "We'll talk to her. Then we'll talk to Riley and tell him everything, and I mean everything, we think we know."

"I wonder how many other women they were blackmailing?" Linda mused. "Any one of them could have reached the end of her rope and killed Liz. Maybe someone just snapped." Her lips curled up faintly. "The more victims we find, the more suspects the police will have."

I knew there was a flaw in that logic somewhere. I just had to find it before we questioned every woman in the gym. That could land us in hot water with a lot of people other than Riley Furman.

We hightailed it out, skipping the post-exercise shower. We were concentrating on avoiding all the piercing stares targeted at us, which was why I wasn't looking where I was going and collided with a solid object, losing my balance. Arms reached out to keep me from falling. I looked up into a pair of familiar gray eyes. It was Riley Furman. "What are you doing here?" he asked.

"We were working out," I replied, stretching my spandex clad body to its full five feet five inches in height. For a moment I thought I saw appreciation in his eyes. Then he started to scowl again. Why did he keep doing that?

"Hmhmm," he said, sliding his eyes to his companion. It was the woman I'd seen him with at the house. She eyed us skeptically, one hand on a hip. "Why don't you go on ahead?" he said to her. She nodded, studying each of us carefully as though memorizing our faces before heading into the gym.

Maybe it was just as well we hadn't showered. Our slightly sweaty smell might convince the police that we were innocent of anything other than getting in shape.

"We need to talk," Furman said, guiding me by the elbow to a bench by the entrance. My friends started to follow, but he held up a peremptory hand.

"Truth," he said. He tried to get me to sit down but I resisted. I wasn't falling for that power positioning stuff.

Riley sighed. "Mrs. Olsen," he began.

"Jackie."

"Jackie, do you remember our conversation the other day?"

"A conversation has more than once side," I said, crossing my arms. "I remember an inquisition and a lecture."

He sighed again. "Please don't make this difficult. What are you doing here?"

I tried to maintain my story but his gray eyes were really penetrating. It felt as if he could read my mind. "We were checking out something our children told us," I blurted.

He cocked an eyebrow. I glanced at my buddies, who had snuck close enough to hear what we were saying. They nodded as one, although Marcia looked unhappy about doing so. I spilled my guts, about what Nick and Max had told me, about the steroids, about the women at the gym and their behavior, about our conjectures. I remembered our vote and didn't mention the redhead.

"The boys didn't have any proof," I finished. "It didn't make sense to call you and waste your time. And we had no idea Adam Wright might be having dalliances with some of the women he coaches. We still don't know that for sure."

"You didn't have proof positive, so you decided to investigate on your own," he finished for me.

I nodded, gulping and feeling guilty. There would be no more votes, I vowed. I slid my eyes to Marcia who stared innocently back. "I guess you had some ideas Adam was up to something," I said.

He studied my face. "We heard some rumors." A small smile tugged at his mouth. There was that dimple again. It sure was appealing. "But you've given us some new avenues to explore." He took me by my shoulders. "Nonetheless, what I said at your house stands. Leave the investigating to us. You could get hurt. So could your friends." He gave them a cold cop glare. Then he squeezed my shoulders slightly. My entire body tingled. Riley stepped back. The stern face reappeared. "You could also screw up our investigation. That would be a problem. Possibly a big one." I thought back to my conversation with Jeremy Barber. So much for tingling, at least the kind I had been feeling a moment ago. My current tingling was not good. It was not good at all. However, I didn't appreciate what seemed to be a threat. I scowled right back at him.

"Go home, Miss Marple," Riley said. He made a sweeping gesture. "All of you go home."

We watched silently as his partner marched Adam Wright to their waiting car.

CHAPTER THIRTEEN

"I don't know if I'll ever be able to show my face at the gym again," Bernice moaned. She jiggled the ice cubes in her glass of tea.

"Why would you want to?" I asked. She, Marcia and Linda looked perplexed. "I'm serious," I said, spreading my hands out in front of me. "That place is one huge soap opera. I mean, you have sex, drugs – all you need is rock and roll, to paraphrase an old saying."

"The gym has all the latest equipment," Linda protested.

"It has some great programs and classes too," Marcia added.

"One thing that bugged me," I continued, ignoring their protests, "was how self occupied the people seemed to be. I was watching and to a person they were looking at themselves in the mirrors. Everyone was admiring their own perfect body. It seemed more competitive than friendly. If you're not a professional athlete, why would you want to work out in that kind of atmosphere?" I took a sip of tea. "I still say that if I were going to join a gym, which I am not, I would go to the YMCA. They have loads of great equipment, plenty of people to help when you need it, and a terrific water aerobics program. That's much more my style."

"You have a point," Linda admitted. "I hadn't noticed all that was going on in the background. I may check the Y out. As to the spa treatments, I really like the Urban Escape Spa on Winter Street."

"This conversation is leading us nowhere," Marcia said gloomily. "I fully expect our gym memberships to be revoked after today in any event."

Linda spread a piece of paper open on my dining room table. We leaned forward to study it. "After our adventure I snuck back into the gym," she said. "I managed to charm Teddy into getting

me a list of all of Adam Wright's clients."
"How did you do that?" I was impressed.
"Apparently seeing Adam escorted out by the police freaked him out. He wants to help Lexie and Dan too. Also, it turns out Adam isn't popular with some of the staff," Linda said. "Teddy said he had no problem getting what I wanted."
"Is Adam still working at the gym?"? I asked. "I thought that after the police picked him up the gym might let him go."
"Nope," Bernice said. "He wasn't charged with anything and his clients like him, so at least for now he's staying. I have a feeling he's on a short leash, though."
"What about the steroids?" I asked.
"No proof," Bernice said shortly.
"At least not yet," Marcia contributed.
"And sexual relations with his clients?"
"Once again, no proof."
"After Lisa what's-her-name slaps him silly in front of how many clients?"
"I suspect Adam will be gone soon. The manager is probably going to ask around and I suspect somebody will spill the beans, at least about the sex. Adam will want to move to a new employer before he's fired," Linda said.
Marcia growled again. "That guy has more hands than an octopus. I thought he was just plain creepy. And no one touches me like that but my Bob." Marcia smiled beatifically. And when he does, we..."
Bernice slapped her hands over her ears. "TMI!"
"But you really should try..."
"No!" Linda said. "Stop! Now!"
Marcia pouted, running her fingers through her green-tipped spikes. "Your loss."
"Oh, honey, you don't know," Bernice said lasciviously.
"Enough, already!" I protested. "Some of us are living like nuns. I don't need to hear this."
"I bet that could change," Marcia said. "That detective said he was watching you. I bel he'd like to do more than that."

"Ladies!" I slammed my hands on the table. "Focus!"

They jumped. I pointed to the list. "What about Mrs. Leopard Spandex?"

"Cleo?" Bernice snorted. "She'd tell Liz she could take out a front page ad as far as Cleo was concerned. The woman is incorrigible."

"Amanda Wilkinson is a different matter," Linda said, tapping the paper with a manicured nail. "She's a poster child for a trophy wife. Her husband is considerably older than she is, very wealthy, and concerned with his social standing and reputation. I'd be willing to bet there's a prenup there. She gets caught, she loses everything." Bernice put a checkmark by the name.

We continued through the list. Among them Marcia, Linda and Bernice knew all the women. I only knew a couple. My friends were right. I needed to get out more.

One of the names on the list belonged to a young woman my friends believed to be an abused wife.

"She might be susceptible to someone who seems gentle and concerned," Linda mused. "And she might attack Liz out of fear of her husband."

Check.

"Adam Wright is a pig," Marcia pronounced. No argument there.

At the end of the exercise, four names were checked off in addition to red headed Lisa.

I pointed to the name of a woman I knew. "Let me talk to her. We know each other fairly well. At one point she was having some marital problems, so she could certainly be a candidate. I can't imagine her harming a fly, but anything's possible."

"I remember talking to the woman we think was being abused a few times," Linda said. "I'll tackle her."

"Amanda Wilkinson is a tough cookie," Bernice said. "I think it's going to take team work to get anything out of her."

Marcia pointed to Lisa's name. "I still think we need to start there."

"How are we going to do that?" I asked.

She gave us a crafty smile. "Listen and learn, ladies. Listen and learn." Why did the rest of us look worried?

Actually, Marcia set up a meeting with Lisa with relative ease. She dialed her number and jumped right into her spiel. "Lisa, this is Marcia from the gym. I feel so awful about what happened today. Are you all right?" Apparently, she received a one-word answer. "We've been hearing stories about Adam Wright. In fact, I don't know if you saw where he put his hands on me today. And he was definitely looking down Linda's top. She was really creeped out when he wouldn't stop staring."

Linda raised her eyebrows. "I was?" she mouthed.

"I'm calling because we need to do something about him. We thought we could get together and talk about it. And if there's anything we can do to help you feel better, we'd like to do that to." Marcia listened a moment and then she laughed. "Yes, unfortunately we love fattening stuff. Tomorrow morning at Franco's Bakery sounds great. We'll see you at 9:00." She hung up the phone triumphantly. "We have a breakfast date." We all did a high five.

The following morning we gathered at Franco's. I am happy to report that none of us were wearing spandex. Franco's was a European style bakery and restaurant that served amazing breakfast pastries and some of the best cappuccino you could find anywhere. Inside French music played softly in the background. Why French music and an Italian name? No one knew. We put it down as eclectic. The walls were taupe and black vertical stripes with black and white pictures of European cities for decoration. A glass case filled with sugary pastries and savory quiches and pies lined one wall. The waiters wore black slacks and white dress shirts covered by long aprons tied at the waist. Glass covered tables and wrought iron chairs completed the scene.

Lisa was sitting at a corner table, sipping a cappuccino and leafing through a magazine when we arrived. We all sat, exchanged pleasantries and placed our orders. I practically salivated when our waiter delivered my pastry, an airy confection topped with whipped cream and fresh raspberries.

Lisa sat back and surveyed us. "I'm not sure this is such a good idea." She pointed at Marcia, Linda and Bernice. "I've remembered that you were friends of Liz Williams." She looked me over. "I assume you were too. Well, it turns out Liz was no friend of mine, so I see no reason to talk to you."

That wasn't an auspicious start.

"Then why did you come?" Bernice asked.

Lisa shrugged. "Curiosity more than anything I suppose. Liz was murdered, you were her friends and I decided to find out what you really want with me."

"We really would like to see Adam Wright get in trouble," Marcia assured her. "It looks to us like he's taking advantage of women at the gym and that needs to stop."

"Why not just report him?" Lisa asked.

"And say what?" Marcia replied. "I wasn't happy with the way he touched me? He looked down Linda's top?"

Lisa looked at Linda. "Were you really creeped out?"

Linda smiled back at her. "Can't say I liked it, but unfortunately it's nothing unusual."

"Your friend was in cahoots with Adam," Lisa said. "Why should I talk with you? As a matter of fact, why should I trust you?"

Bernice leaned forward. "We knew Liz a long time. The Liz we saw in the past six months or so wasn't the sweet, loveable person we knew. We keep hearing rumors about her being involved in some very bad things and wonder whether any of them got her killed. Right now the police seem focused on her husband and daughter, and we can't believe they're guilty. If we could figure out what Liz was up to, maybe that would give the police some more suspects."

Lisa narrowed her eyes at her. "I would think they'd already be looking."

"They probably are," I admitted. "But sometimes people tell friends things they wouldn't tell a detective or an investigator. We thought that if you could tell us what you meant about Liz yesterday it would give us some ideas and we could approach the police without having to involve you."

Lisa sipped her coffee. "You won't give the police my name?"
"We can't promise that," I admitted. "We'll do our best not to involve you. That's the best we can do."
Lisa thought a moment and then nodded her head decisively, leaning forward, hands circling her cup. "I made a terrible mistake," she said. "My husband and I were going through a tough time. I was upset all the time and didn't know what to do. I was sure we were going to get divorced. I didn't want that and I was so distraught I needed to talk to someone."
"And so?" Bernice said encouragingly.
"I talked to Adam." Lisa laughed bitterly. "He was so concerned, so caring, such a good listener. One thing led to another and..." she bit her lip, "I slept with him." She blinked back tears. "As soon as I did it I regretted it. What a way to save my marriage, huh?" We all made sympathetic noises. "A couple weeks later Liz approached me at the gym. She told me she knew I'd had sex with Adam. She threatened to tell my husband unless I gave her money."
"How much?" I asked.
The tears rolled down her cheeks. "$500. I did it. I thought that was the end of it. But she came back again."
"And you paid her?" Linda asked.
Lisa nodded. "She came back a third time, but the next thing I knew she was dead."
"Oh, honey," Marcia said, pulling out tissues for both of them. "I'm so sorry that happened." She covered Lisa's hand with her own.
Bernice was frowning and Linda looked disgusted. There were tears in my eyes also.
"Do you know anyone else this happened to?" I asked.
Lisa shook her head. "Not for sure. I suspect Amanda Wilkinson might have been in the same boat, but I'm not sure." She took a deep breath and gave a tremulous smile. "You know, it does feel good to tell someone."
"How's your marriage now?" Bernice asked.
"It's better. One day at a time. We both want to stay together so

we're working on it. We're seeing a counselor and I have hope." She eyed my pastry. "Could I have a bite of that?"

"Let me buy you your own," I said. "It's time for someone to treat you to something sweet." Lisa whispered her thanks.

"And don't try to work that off at the gym," Linda said sternly. We all laughed.

We left Lisa and stood by our cars.

"That was truly awful," Linda said, "but at this point I couldn't say it was a surprise."

Bernice sighed.

Marcia shook her head. "I hope we took some weight off her shoulders."

"I hope we don't have to tell the cops," I said.

We stood in silence for a moment.

"Well," Bernice said, "I'm off to see what I can find out about our abused wife."

"Maggie and I are going to meet my friend," I said.

"And I'm going to try to get a meeting with Amanda Wilkinson," Linda said. "Remind me how I got that job?"

"Just lucky, I guess" Marcia said, punching her on the shoulder.

The woman I had been assigned had a gorgeous standard poodle who had been in Maggie's puppy class. Already he could shake paws, heel (some of the time) and sit. Maggie remained a work in progress although she could do all of those things and more, thank you, when she felt like it or when a treat was involved. When no treats were involved, all bets were off.

The four of us often met at the dog park for a play date. My friend was only too happy to agree to a time and we now sat on a very uncomfortable bench in 80-degree weather watching our pups frolic.

"This has been a weird few weeks," my friend said before I could start a conversation. Thank goodness! I really didn't want to be an inquisitor.

"Really? Maggie, stop that!" She seemed to be using Zeus' ear for a chew toy.

"I've been working with a personal trainer," she said.

"No kidding? What's that like?" Her abdomen did look flatter and her upper arms in that sleeveless top looked great. Maybe I *should* reconsider the gym.

"A couple weeks ago he hit on me."

"Are you kidding?" I faced her straight on.

"No, Zeus! Don't eat that!" The poodle turned his head, looked her in the eye and swallowed whatever was in his mouth whole. She laughed. "I mean, he started telling me how great I looked, then he got more forward, rubbing my shoulders and...and other places."

I held my breath.

"Things haven't been that great between Joe and me. I think you know that." She shook her head. "Did you ever cheat on Lars?"

I was taken aback. "What? Me? No, never!" I never would...I loved him," I said.

My friend gave me a glorious smile. "I thought about doing something with this guy and all of a sudden I thought 'What in the world are you thinking? You love Joe. He loves you. So what if things aren't all wine and roses? Fix it.' So we did. We changed our routine. We're having date nights, the kids are going to their grandparents for sleepovers and," she lowered her voice to a whisper, "the sex has never been better!" Scratch one off the list.

When my friends and I got back together only one name remained on the list. Obviously, the name of my dog park friend was absent. Another woman freely admitted to an affair. Liz had approached her, but as the woman had no spouse or significant other, she sent Liz packing.

Bernice had learned that the abused wife had reported Adam to his supervisor for making sexual overtures and moved to Colorado to be closer to her sister and brother-in-law, who had long been worried about her. We wished her luck. "Why didn't the supervisor do anything?" Bernice fretted.

"Happens all the time," said Linda, our representative in the corporate world.

"So that leaves us with Amanda Wilkinson," said Marcia.

"Yes, and we're having drinks with her this evening," Linda said.

"Oh, lucky us," said Bernice.

CHAPTER FOURTEEN

With a height of seven stories, the Majestic Hotel is the closest thing Summer Hill has to a skyscraper. The name majestic suits it well. It is an ornate art nouveau beauty built near the turn of the century. As you enter from the sidewalk you are greeted by two massive doors into which are set pieces of glass that curve toward each other at the top of gently sloping sides. Each pane of glass is decorated with a tableau of nature. On the right is a scene depicting a regal stork standing in a pond of high grasses and water lilies. The left pane shows a proud male peacock, tail spread in front of him showing off its bright hues of blue and green. When you enter the lobby it is hard to know where to look first. If you look down you see an intricate mosaic floor that manages to include Greek key design with flowing naturalistic ornamentation. As you look up your eyes seem to search for the sky, as a glass dome of blues and greens reaches two stories to the ceiling, centered by a round stained glass composition depicting nymphs playing on a river bank. In the center of the lobby stands a semicircular reception desk with copper ornamentation. To either side statues of nymphs spring from fountains. The lobby holds a variety of chairs and couches arranged in conversation groupings. A remarkable collection of lamps designed by such luminaries as Louis Comfort Tiffany and Emile Galle grace the side tables. One would expect this combination of color and form to be overwhelming, but somehow it comes together in a vibrant whole and is, well, majestic.

The owners of the hotel have created an open air bar on the roof of the hotel. Unlike the lobby the bar is very modern and hip, and has become 'the' place to meet for cocktails and appetizers. I had never been. Lars and I had the bar on our list of places to visit, but somehow never managed to do so. The thought made my heart give a slight twinge. In spite of this memory, I would have been excited to visit the bar if it weren't for Amanda Wilkinson's reputation for unpleasantness.

When we emerged onto the roof from the elevator we took time to look around. The roof had been divided into rooms by the clever use of concrete plant containers that were home to lush evergreens and perennials. Bright annuals lent splashes of color. To one end was a fire pit, to the other a tranquil lap pool filled with water lilies. From the roof you could see the streets and rooftops of our main commercial area and spot tables at the multiple restaurants and cafes. To the west spread Lake Summer, the centerpiece of the city's park, which allowed for many outdoor recreational pleasures such as kayaking, walking, jogging, and playing tennis.

We surveyed the occupants of the bar. There was no sign of Amanda. "That's not surprising," Linda said. "She likes to make an entrance."

"Assuming she comes at all," Bernice said. "It would be like her to stand us up."

"At least let's have a cocktail," Marcia said. "I hear the bartenders can whip up some wonderful concoctions."

We had just ordered when the elevator doors once again opened and Amanda Wilkinson stepped onto the roof. She gave us a wave and walked toward us as though she were the star of a fashion show.

"I never walked like that when I was I model," Bernice muttered under her breath. "Talk about overdone."

"It's getting attention," Linda said. "Isn't that what it's all about?"

Marcia stood up and air kissed Amanda on each cheek. "How nice to see you. Sit down and let us buy you a drink."

Amanda sat and crossed her legs, exposing a large swath of thigh. She raised her hand to attract our waiter and ordered a dirty martini. After placing her order she surveyed our group. She leaned forward and extended her hand to me. "I don't believe we've met."

"I'm Jackie Olsen. The four of us are neighbors."

Amanda gave a smile that didn't reach her eyes. "I suppose you

were a neighbor of Liz Williams also then."
"I lived next door."
The waiter delivered her drink and she took a sip. "Living on the same street where a murder was committed must be fascinating." She tossed her hair and the one carat solitaires on her earlobes caught the light. For that matter, so did the humongous diamond on her left hand and those on her clunky tennis bracelet. Amanda leaned forward. "Tell me more."
I was startled. The word fascinating was an odd choice. I would have expected someone to say terrifying, horrible, upsetting or a variety of other words. But fascinating?
I glanced at Bernice, who pulled her mouth to one side in a grimace. Linda and Marcia both seemed to be looking for something in their drink glasses. I took a sip of my own cocktail. "I'm not sure what you want me to say," I admitted. "I was one of the people who found Liz's body and it was the worst experience of my life."
Amanda looked taken aback. Good. After a moment she ostentatiously raised her arm and looked at her Rolex. "Why don't you ladies tell me why we're here?" Amanda said. "I don't have much time. I'm meeting Charles for dinner."
"Why do *you* think we're here?" Marcia asked.
Amanda leaned back in her seat. "It's obvious, isn't it? You want to take over where Liz left off."
"I confess I don't have the slightest idea what you're talking about." Linda motioned for another round of drinks.
"You don't?" Amanda lifted a perfectly shaped eyebrow. She smiled again. This time I decided she looked like a shark.
Amanda sucked on an olive from her martini and sat forward. "Oh, come on, ladies. You know Liz was blackmailing me and you want to do the same."
Marcia managed to look shocked. "We want to do no such thing."
Amanda looked at her watch again. "Then what in the world do you want?"
Bernice spoke up. "Just tell us how Liz was blackmailing you and why."

Amanda re-crossed her legs. “You don’t want money?”
We all shook our heads.
“Fine. I had an affair with Adam Wright.” No surprise there. “Let’s agree that he‘s a very attractive man. Let’s also acknowledge that my husband is twenty years older than I am. He’s charming and debonair and believe it or not I enjoy his company. He’s not bad in bed, but I wanted someone who was…shall we say …a little more adventurous.”
“And Liz found out.”
Amanda snorted. “Found out? Adam told her, the worm. And he gave her some very embarrassing photos. How he took those I don’t know, but that doesn’t matter. Liz asked for money. I paid her.”
“How much?” I asked.
“Does it matter?” Amanda asked. “Oh, never mind. $5000.”
I must have gasped.
Amanda waved her hand as though swatting a gnat. “I can afford it. Charles gives me a very generous allowance.”
“She kept coming back, didn’t she?” Linda asked.
“Yes. She was very annoying. I knew I was going to have to put my foot down. But then she was murdered. And here we are.” She gave a brilliant smile and I could see how some would men would find that attractive. My friends and I remained silent. Marcia drained her glass. Linda did the same.
Amanda surveyed our group again. “And why *are* we here?” She squinted at us, threw her head back and laughed. “My God, you think I killed Liz! That’s funny.” We didn’t laugh with her.
Amanda rose. “Ladies, if I murdered Liz I would have slipped poison into her wine glass, not stabbed her. How incredibly messy. Now, if you’ll excuse me, I’m going to join my husband for dinner.” She sashayed toward to elevator, causing every male eye to follow her departing form.
We all watched her as well. I cogitated a moment. “I’ve thought of something,” I said after an appropriate time of meditation.
My friends turned bleak faces toward me. “Next to Liz was an overturned table together with two glasses and a bottle of wine.”

Linda frowned. "And therefore?"

"Amanda seems to have known Liz was a wine drinker. How many others knew that?"

"So, Amanda may have been at the house that night and killed her. They argued and things got violent," Marcia contributed.

Bernice nodded. "Or she thought she was meeting with a friend."

My head was spinning from our conversation with Amanda Wilkinson, let alone the two cocktails I'd consumed. After I got home I downed a couple glasses of water along with a preventative aspirin. The floor stopped moving and I decided to take Maggie for a walk in the park. I hooked up her leash and we headed out on our favorite trail that skirted the lake edge, moved through a shaded area filled with mountain laurel and rhododendrons and ended up near the tennis courts.

I was deep in thought when I heard something moving in the bushes on the side of the path. A hand reached out and jerked me off the trail, pulling my arm so hard that I lost my grip on Maggie's leash. Whoever it was spun me around and put his hand under my chin, squeezing my throat. "You bitch!" I looked into the eyes of Adam Wright. "You ratted me out to the police! You've ruined my life. I'm going to kill you."

Out of the corner of my eye I saw a tan blur. Maggie, all teeth and claws, grabbed hold of Adam's leg. He shook his leg viciously and she went flying, landing with a yelp on the ground. Maggie's attack caused him to loosen his grip slightly. I managed to scream before his hand once again closed on my throat. I struggled, trying to remember every self defense trick I had ever learned. I clawed at his face, ripping the skin off his cheeks, managing to turn and aim for his eyes. I fought like a demon and stomped as hard as I could on his ankle. Maggie attacked again and held on for dear life. He sent her flying just as I heard footsteps thundering toward us.

"Hey, you! Stop it!" Two young men with the physiques of line backers plowed into Adam and he fell forward, almost taking me with him. I heard other female voices screaming along with mine. I struggled out of Adam's grip as my rescuers struggled to subdue him.

A woman in a jogging outfit ran up, holding her cell phone. “I called 911!”

Adam continued to struggle. The jogger yanked a can from her shorts pocket and pepper sprayed him in the face. Now he was screaming in agony. In the periphery of my vision I saw a streak of blue. A uniformed policeman was kneeling on Adam’s prostrate form, cuffing his hands behind his back.

I collapsed on the grass, struggling to take in air. My throat was on fire. “My puppy!” I managed to gasp. “My puppy?” I was crying.

“She’s fine.” A young woman knelt on the grass beside me. “Here she is.” She placed Maggie in my lap and the dog licked my face as I frantically felt her body for injury.

I heard more running footsteps and someone threw himself in front of me, gathering Maggie and me into his arms. Whoever it was stroked my hair and murmured over and over “It’s all right. It’s all right.” I looked up into the gray eyes of Riley Furman.

About an hour later I sat in my living room surrounded by my friends. Nick sat on the floor and cuddled Maggie in his lap. He had rushed her to the emergency veterinary clinic and had been assured that other than being bruised and having a chipped tooth Maggie would be fine. She was exhausted and after a valiant attempt to stay awake had fallen asleep and was softly snoring.

I was nursing a glass of whiskey, which Marcia assured me would ease the pain in my throat. I couldn’t follow her logic, as my injuries were external, but I was in no shape to argue.

Ray and Bob sat in stunned silence as they learned what their wives had been up to.

“So why was Riley Furman there?” I whispered. That seemed to be the best I could do. My throat really hurt. In fact, it felt like it was on fire. Marcia pressed a little more alcohol on me. "Take this, it really will help," she said.

I hesitated, thinking I had already reached my limit of alcohol consumption for the day, but after a moment I complied. I sipped the whiskey. Marcia was right. It seemed to desensitize my bruised throat. Swallowing was less difficult. Of course, at the same time my brain was starting to feel like a piece of fuzzy cotton.

"He heard the call on his radio and was in the area," Bernice answered.

"He was so shocked I thought he might pass out," Linda volunteered. "I suspect your next conversation isn't going to be pleasant."

Ray shook his head. "Enough, ladies. Enough. You can't keep meddling in this case. Let it go."

Bob nodded decisively. "I'm going to chain you to a chair if you keep this up," he said to his wife.

Marcia cooed. "Ooh, that would be something new."

We couldn't help but laugh. I looked at my friends' faces. They were frightened. They were scared. They were determined.

I had a feeling Bob and Ray weren't going to get their way. My friends intended to continue their quest to save Lexie and Dan from the policemen's snares. And now they were determined to protect me.

CHAPTER FIFTEEN

It would be an understatement to say that my next encounter with Riley Furman was stressful. I awoke at 7:00 in the morning to hear someone repeatedly pressing my doorbell. It had to be the detective. I groaned and pulled my pillow over my head. Liz's funeral was that afternoon. After the previous night the last thing I needed was an encounter of the worst kind with an irate police officer before seeing my friend laid to rest. My throat still hurt and I was suffering the effects of Marcia's alcohol driven remedy. How much of that stuff did I drink anyway? I suspected I didn't want to know. My eyes were crusted with sleeper's dust. I had the world's worst breath. I burrowed further under my covers. Maybe if I played dead Riley Furman would go away. I pressed the pillow closer to my ears and remained steadfast in my resolve not to answer the door.

Unfortunately, Nick was made of lesser stuff. I heard him pad to the door and open it. "My mom's sleeping," he informed Furman.

"Then get her up," he growled. Of all the nerve! Unless he had come to arrest me I had no intention of budging.

"Mom?" Nick poked his head into my room. "Detective Furman is here."

"Tell him to go away," I grumbled.

"He's already in the house," Nick said. "He's making a cup of coffee."

I cursed the ease with which Furman had made himself at home. I struggled out of bed and jumped into the shower. Deciding to let him wait I applied makeup and carefully chose my new pink spandex tights and tunic top. Instead of putting on the coordinating headband I fluffed my hair alluringly and applied styling mousse. After making my bed I was out of excuses not to leave my room. Maybe I'd be lucky and Riley would be gone.

Of course, I had no such luck. He was sitting at the kitchen table with the newspaper spread in front of him. He had loosened his tie and removed his jacket so that his holstered gun was prominently visible. Maggie was sitting at his feet and he appeared to be feeding her treats from the jar on the counter. From the way she was looking at him I could tell she had fallen in love. I watched him for a moment. He really did look quite comfortable sitting in my kitchen. In fact, he looked as though he belonged there. Now that was an alarming thought.

"Good morning."

Riley turned and ran his eyes over my body. They seemed to be crackling with emotion, probably anger. "I have been poring over the state statutes trying to find a way to take you into custody," he said. Never mind morning pleasantries.

I sat demurely on the couch, hands in my lap and legs crossed at the ankle, just like we were taught in etiquette classes.

Riley started pacing the living room like a caged lion. How can someone sound like they're yelling when in reality they are speaking quite softly? In some ways it was more menacing than a good old fashioned shouting match would have been. "I've even talked with the District Attorney about naming you as a material witness and taking you into protective custody." I watched him pace and said nothing.

He stopped pacing and stalked up to the couch. Finally he yelled. "Good God, woman, do you realize how close you came to being killed last night?"

I jumped. "Yes." I whispered. "I was just..."

"Just what?" Riley asked softly.

"Just walking my dog."

He threw his hands up in the air. "And thank goodness you have her!" he said. He paused to scratch Maggie's ears and slip her another treat. "This dog deserves a medal." He pondered for a minute. "Maggie could have been killed too," he said.

The tears started. At first they rolled slowly down my cheeks. I thought about losing my precious pup and cried harder. I thought about Liz and sobbed uncontrollably. Riley looked dumbstruck.

Nick ran back into the room. "Mom?" He threw a venomous glare at the detective, threw himself on the couch and put his arms around me. "What did you do to her?"

"I didn't do anything," Riley protested, taking a step closer.

"Just stay where you are!" Nick commanded. "You leave my mother alone. You're a bully. Go away."

I had largely regained my posture although my breath was coming in deep hiccups. Riley grabbed a paper towel from the roll in the kitchen and thrust it at me. "I'm not a bully," he muttered. He sat on my other side, trying to ignore my irate son. "I tried to warn you, Jackie," he said more gently. "I didn't know Adam would go after you, but I was afraid something bad could happen with you and your buddies poking your noses into everything."

"Where's Adam now?"

"He's in jail," the detective said grimly. "If I have anything to do with it he's going to stay there."

I blew my nose. "Won't he get out on bail?"

Riley held out his hand for my soggy towel. "Not if I can help it." He threw the paper in the trash. "Do you want a cup of coffee? He peered at the selections for my single cup brewing machine. "Maybe tea? How about hot chocolate?"

Nick had released his hold on me but was eyeing the detective suspiciously.

"Tea would be nice."

"I'll make it." Nick walked to the kitchen. "I know how she likes it." I watched my sixteen-year-old man of the house and teared up all over.

'Oh, Lars,' I thought, "Where are you when we need you?'

Riley handed me another towel.

"We have some muffins," I said. "I made them last night. They're Nick's favorites, raspberry and almond. Would you like a couple?"

"That would be nice," Riley said, "if you're having one."

I stood. "Tell you what. Let's all have breakfast." I tied an apron around my waist and took bacon and eggs out of the refrigerator.

"I make a pretty mean omelet," Furman said. "Would you guys

like that?" I nodded, Nick shrugged and Riley rummaged around in the refrigerator.

Half an hour we were all sitting at the table. The omelet, filled with spinach and cheese, smelled fantastic. The bacon was crisp as it should be, the orange juice freshly squeezed.

"So about Adam Wright," Riley said, washing a piece of muffin down with his second cup of coffee. "I think we have him to rights on selling illegal steroids."

I was surprised. "How did that happen?"

He gave a half smile. "It was largely due to your friend Teddy. I convinced him to get a bunch of the college athletes together with a promise nothing bad would happen to them. Then I explained the long-term effect of steroids on, uh, certain parts of their anatomy."

I didn't have the slightest idea what he was talking about.

"They make your testicles shrink," Nick said. I choked on my tea. Where did he get this information? And was Riley blushing?

"Having something wrong with your sexual organs is an adolescent male's worst nightmare," he explained. "In no time we had one of the prescriptions. I paid a visit to the doctor whose name was on the pad."

"Another of Adam's conquests?" I guessed.

He nodded. "She swears he must have stolen the prescription pads. We'll figure out whether she's lying later. That, combined with the attack on you last night should make any reasonable judge deny bail. Fortunately, the DA has charged Adam with everything she can think of, including attempted murder and animal abuse. I doubt he'll be going anywhere for a long time."

He looked at a gadget hooked onto his belt, stood up and tossed his napkin on the table. "I'd like to help with clean up but I have to go. I'm sorry."

"No problem." I waved a hand toward the door.

Riley's gray eyes fixed on mine. "The funeral is this afternoon," he said. "Can I trust you not to get into trouble?"

"Absolutely," I assured him. He didn't look convinced as he left.

Nick was a pallbearer at Liz's funeral, as were Marcia's twins,

Dan's brother and, of all people, Lexie's former boyfriend. Nick informed me that the young man had broken up with the cheerleader and was trying to get back with Lexie but that, at least according to Nick, 'she wasn't having it.'

Behind me Nick cleared his throat. He stood in the doorway, self conscious in the suit we had bought for the occasion. The suit jacket was long and tapered, accenting his broad shoulders and narrow hips. His blonde hair was attractively tousled and his blue eyes shone behind the dark-rimmed glasses he had elected to wear over his contact lenses, thinking they made him look more serious.

I felt tears pool in my eyes. He was almost seventeen. In no time he'd be off to college. Once again he looked so much like his father. I felt so bad Lars wasn't at my side. And I felt terrible for Dan and Lexie. I patted Maggie, who was dancing anxiously around our ankles sensing tension. "Let's go," I said, taking a deep breath. Nick secured Maggie in her crate and we headed toward the church.

We carpooled with Linda, as Marcia and Bernice were driving to the church with their respective families. Linda looked sharp in one of her beautifully tailored business suits, not a hair out of place as always.

I had gone shopping in my closet, finally choosing a taupe pencil skirt with a patterned blouse and black jacket. I had pulled my hair back in a chignon, pulling a few tendrils loose to frame my face. A jet necklace and matching earrings completed the ensemble. Fortunately the necklace helped conceal the bruises on my neck. I slid my feet into ridiculously high heels, pleased to note that they made my legs, toned by daily walking, look long and sleek. Not bad, if I did say so myself. But what did it matter? Today wasn't about me. Also, it wasn't as if I was dressing for anyone special, although there was a chance I'd run into Riley Furman, or possibly another interesting man.

Although we arrived early the parking lot was nearly full. St. Stephen's is a large granite building constructed in the 1800's. It sits in the heart of Summer Hill's historic district (almost every town in Virginia has one). Its bell tower soars toward the sky, creating the focal point for the front of the church. Today the bells were softly pealing, inviting us to worship.

The church's claim to fame is its series of stained glass windows designed and made by Tiffany. The windows run down either side of the building and a magnificent rose window glows at the rear of the church. When the sun shines, as it was today, the windows are a sight to behold, gleaming with an ethereal light. I'd studied the artwork and every year served as a docent during the church's annual fair. The windows never failed to impress me and with the sun streaming through the glass it felt like the church actually contained a small piece of Heaven.

The building is fronted by a large perennial garden where early roses were already blooming. We recently added a maze for meditation walks with a magnolia surrounded by stone benches in the center. Often you'll find people walking the circle, meditating, or reading spiritual tomes. Today it was empty.

Behind the church is a large graveyard where Liz was to be buried. The graveyard pre-exists the church and there are fascinating graves and monuments dating to the 1700's. One can spend happy hours just browsing, but not on a day with a funeral, although people sometimes wander off after the event.

Nick, normally adverse to public displays of affection from his mother, gave me a quick hug before leaving to join his fellow pallbearers.

The tears started again as I watched him join a cluster of dark suited youth. Linda took my hand and we walked that way into the church. I noticed that she was blinking rapidly and her eyes were none too dry either.

The church was packed. I recognized neighbors, teachers, people from the gym and some students. It seemed that most of Lexie's class had turned out, some with their parents, others sitting in two or threes, along with a couple larger groups who may have been members of the swim and tennis teams. Some of their faces looked familiar. I wondered if the mean girls were there. If so, they were on their best behavior. I didn't see anyone glued to a phone, or observe any whispering or giggling. Ms. Sherwood, whom I knew from volunteering, gave me a small smile of recognition. I shot her a surreptitious thumbs up and her smile widened.

Finally I spied Bernice and Marcia, seated near the front with their spouses. Bernice was her normal gorgeous self. Marcia's hair was actually its natural color and was combed into a demure pixie style. She wore a conservative polka dot dress and looked every bit the average suburban housewife. What a chameleon.

The organist began to play and the family trooped in. I was shocked when I saw Dan. He looked like he'd aged 10 years, his face slack and his eyes glazed, walking slumped rather than with his normal ramrod posture. His sister walked next to him, her arm around his waist. Lexie followed, sandwiched between her grandparents. She'd obviously been crying and was clutching a wad of face tissue. Her grandmother, thin lipped and grim faced, walked slightly in front of her, staring straight ahead. Her grandfather, whom I remembered as a kind and gentle man, walked behind Lexie, acknowledging friends with a faint tip of his chin. What were their names? I'd need to remember for the reception. Tom and Adele, that was it. I breathed a mental sigh of relief. At least I wouldn't be embarrassed by forgetting their names at an awkward moment.

Liz's siblings and their families followed Dan's family. Her parents had both passed away a few years earlier. That in itself seemed a blessing. I couldn't imagine outliving your child, let alone in circumstances like there.

Ed Scruggs entered the church, clad in the traditional white collar and black shirt of an Episcopal priest. A large cross hung from his neck. He stopped to speak briefly to Dan, resting a hand lightly on his shoulder, then squatted in front of Lexie, taking her hands into his and whispering briefly. Ed climbed into the pulpit and surveyed the congregation. "We are here to celebrate the life of Elizabeth Ann Williams," he began. "Please pray with me." The service was warm and touching. Ed recalled the Liz of old, not the woman she had recently become. He told a couple funny stories about Liz that made even Dan smile in memory. Dan's sister and Liz's brother read from the Scriptures. A soprano sang a magnificent solo, her voice lifting to the timbered rafters. She sang one of Liz's favorite hymns, and it felt to me that Liz's spirit was lifting to Heaven along with the music.

Nick and the other pallbearers lifted Liz's coffin and carried it from the church. Linda and I sobbed. So did many others, including more than a few teenagers.

I was surprised at how many teenagers stayed for the graveside service, which in the Episcopal tradition is short and simple. They probably didn't know they had a choice. As we headed toward the parish hall, however, the crowd began to thin. Nick appeared at my side. I noticed his eyes were red.

"A lot of the kids from school are here," I said inanely as if he hadn't noticed. I hoped Lexie had. Those not leaving seemed to be forming a line to greet the family. I wondered if they knew why they were lining up.

Nick looked around and nodded. "I'm surprised at some of them."

"Why?" I asked.

He shrugged. "Oh, I don't know. Some of them don't really join in much. They don't know Lexie all that well." He pointed to a group of boys clustered to one side. "Them, for example. Those are the brains from our chemistry class. They don't talk much and they're so far ahead of us we probably wouldn't understand them if they did. But they've been going out of their way to be nice to Lexie."

"What about the mean girls?" I was curious.

"They were here but I think they left."

Figures.

The line crept along and suddenly I was face to face with Dan. Before I could say anything he reached out to hug me. I felt him shaking and held him close. He finally broke away. "I'm sorry if I was rough on you the other day."

"Oh, no, Dan, it's all right," I began.

"I got part of my answer," he said.

I looked at him quizzically.

"We had an autopsy done," Dan said. He took a ragged breath. "Liz had a brain tumor. The doctor said it could easily have explained the changes in her personality. If only we had known everything could have been so different."

I hugged him to me again. We were both crying. From further down the line his mother shot me a look of disapproval. To heck with her. This was my friend and he was hurting.

To this day I don't know what I said to the rest of the family. I was in a complete state of shock. Maybe Liz could have been helped. Even if that weren't possible, we all might have reacted differently to her behavior had we known about her illness. We might have been able to stop her from doing some of the things she'd done. She might still be alive. What a burden for a husband to bear. And poor Lexie. Her guilt must feel overwhelming. Ed Scruggs was going to have his work cut out for him. I hoped he was as good a counselor as Ray seemed to think he was.

I was standing near the buffet, staring at nothing, when Adele Williams spoke from behind me. "My son doesn't need a new woman in his life right now."

I started. "Excuse me?"

"You heard what I said," she hissed. "I saw you in the receiving line. Stay away from Dan."

"Mrs. Williams...Adele, I'm Jackie Olsen, Dan's next door neighbor. You and I have met several times. Dan and I have been friends for years. We're not..."

"All the worse!" she snapped. "I want you to leave him alone."

I studied her face. Her mouth was twisted to one side and she was frowning so hard that her eyebrows almost met each other. Clearly this woman was under a tremendous amount of stress. I decided to try to mollify her anger rather than provoke her. "I have no interest in Dan," I said as evenly as I could, "nor does he have any interest in me. Now, if you'll excuse me I'm going to try to forget this conversation ever took place."

As I spoke her shoulders relaxed slightly. I tried to feel sorry for her, but I couldn't help but remember that I had not particularly enjoyed Adele Williams' company when we had been thrown together in social situations. She must have been a monster-in-law rather than a supportive mother-in-law. I felt sorry for Liz. And to think Adele was accusing me of having set my sights on her son at his wife's funeral, of all places!

"Pleasant woman," someone said in my other ear as Adele steamed across the room, shoulders once again stiff and unyielding.

I turned sharply and Riley Furman did a sidestep to avoid spilling the cup of coffee he was holding.

"Sorry," I said, although I really wasn't.

He smiled apologetically. "I shouldn't sneak up on people."

'You shouldn't eavesdrop either,' I thought. I assumed that both habits would be hard for him to break. "So, detectives really do attend funerals."

"Sure. You'd be surprised at what you can pick up."

"Clues?" I asked.

"Depends on what you mean by a clue. More often it's impressions. Amazing what you figure out just by watching people." He sipped his coffee. "And the food is terrific."

I smiled. "You know church ladies. Happy or sad, they cook."

He nodded. "My grandmother was like that. I like it."

"So what have you picked up here?"

He sidestepped the question. "Actually, I'm enjoying watching the kids. It's an awkward age isn't it? Even without the added drama."

I scanned the room. I spied Nick in a corner with some of his friends from the swim team. Man, could those boys eat, no matter the occasion. Elsewhere one of the "brains" chatted up Lexie. She was holding a wadded tissue but was actually smiling. What a sweetheart he must be. I wondered if romance was blooming.

"What group were you in during high school?" the detective asked.

I thought a moment. "The not quites," I finally said.

He raised an inquisitive eyebrow.

"Not quite pretty enough to be majorette, not quite coordinated enough to be a cheerleader, not quite smart enough to be valedictorian."

"Sounds miserable."

"No, I was actually pretty happy. I didn't have the pressures some of those other kids did. I had plenty of friends, played in the band, got tapped for honor society and joined some clubs. All in all, my memories are good."

He tossed his empty cup into the trash and looked me up and down. "I think you look very pretty. You would have made a terrific majorette."

I blushed.

"I don't know about the coordination, but if you can walk in those shoes you must have some. The brains are definitely there. No question about it."

OK. Two could play this game. "What about you?"

To my surprise he took the question seriously. "I was a jock. Not stupid, decent grades, but I lived and breathed baseball." He thought a moment. "In college the brain took over. My parents worked hard to send me. I decided early on I wasn't going to disappoint them."

Maybe that's why he and Teddy had hit it off so well. "What was your major?" I asked.

"History."

That came as a surprise. Why had I expected something less cerebral? Physical education maybe? Possibly I needed to reevaluate this man. "What time period?"

"Middle Ages. Particularly late Middle Ages."

"And you became a detective?"

He grinned. "I got hooked on Cadfael," he said, referring to Derek Jacoby's stellar portrayal of a crime solving monk in the 1100's.

I barked out a short laugh, but quickly clapped my hand over my mouth.

"Besides," Riley continued, "being a cop is better than flipping burgers."

"What's a history major's favorite question?" I asked.

"Do you want fries with that?" we said simultaneously. This time we both laughed, but not too loudly.

"Don't look now, but you're getting the evil eye again," Riley said.

"Oh, for Heaven's sake," I sputtered. I noticed he appeared to be paying attention to me but was actually watching someone over my shoulder. A casual observer wouldn't have noticed.

I held a finger in front of his face. "Hello? I'm over here." His eyes returned to my face. "That's very disconcerting, you know." I said.

"I'm sorry. Occupational hazard."

"Whom were you watching?"

He hesitated. "If you can look without being obvious, tell me if you know the blonde with the French twist. She's wearing a pin-striped suit."

I dropped my napkin and turned in what I hoped was a casual manner as I bent to retrieve it. I spotted an exquisite woman with white blonde hair and bright blue eyes standing alone on the other side of the room. She was a classic Scandinavian beauty, with sculpted cheekbones, even features and a tall, lithe body.

"I've never seen her before. Why?"

"She looks out of place," Riley replied. Obviously I looked confused. "She doesn't seem to know anyone here except Dan. It looks to me like she's wandering around aimlessly and that all her interactions are introductions." He sipped his coffee. "No, I stand corrected. She's talking to a couple of men who seem to know her." His attention didn't shift from the blonde.

"What are you thinking?" I asked.

We watched as the woman approached Dan, putting her hand on his arm. He looked startled and moved slightly away from her touch. "I'm thinking she knows him better than he wants to let on."

My mind shifted back to the telephone conversation I overheard. "Girlfriend possibly?"

"Or more," Furman agreed.

"We could sic Adele on her," I said, referring to Dan's mother.

"No need," the detective said. "I suspect she doesn't need any encouragement."

As we watched Adele approach the unknown blonde, Marcia, Bob in tow, walked up from a different direction and held out her hand.

Riley wrinkled his brow. "She's incorrigible, isn't she? I'll bet she's pumping that woman for information." He let out a long breath. "Didn't last night teach you ladies anything?" He scrutinized Marcia a moment longer.

I chuckled. "Marcia's tenacious," I said, "but she's not stupid. Far from it. She's probably just satisfying her own curiosity. Marcia never met a stranger." As we watched Marcia tucked her hand under the woman's elbow and steered her away from Adele, who looked daggers at them as they walked away.

"Do you like being a detective?" I asked Riley, realizing that I really wanted to know.

He repeated the question thoughtfully. "That's a tough one. On one level, yes. It's challenging, mentally and sometimes physically. And as I told you, often I'm a person's only chance for justice. On the other hand, there's so much tragedy. You see the bad sides of so many people. It can turn you into a terrible cynic if you're not careful."

"Are you a cynic?"

"Sometimes." Now whom was he watching? I looked quickly over my shoulder and realized he was focused on Adele Williams. I spotted his partner on the other side of the room. Her eyes met Riley's and with a slight nod of her head she began to slowly move in Adele's direction.

"I'm starting law school in the fall," the detective said unexpectedly. He was looking directly at me again. "I've always thought being a detective has a shelf life."

"What do you mean?"

"There are limits on how long you can stay sharp enough, quick enough. Slow reflexes can get you killed...or worse. A law degree will give me choices – rise in the ranks, private practice, government work."

"So are you going to quit your job?

"Nah, these days a lot of great schools offer on line courses with short in-classroom requirements."

"What do you think you'll specialize in? Criminal law?"

He shrugged. "Probably, but who knows?"

"You could be a prosecutor," I said.

He shrugged again. "I'm thinking defense."

That was another surprise from him.

"Who knows?" He said. "Maybe I'll fall in love with trusts and estates."

"My husband did," I said.

Riley shot me a sympathetic look. Time to change the subject.

"Did you hear about the autopsy?" I asked.

"The brain tumor?" He nodded. "Damned shame."

"It's tragic. Things could have been so different." The tears started up again. Riley handed me a napkin with a small coffee stain on it. "I'm sorry. I'm an ugly crier." I blew my nose.

"No," he said softly. "I can't imagine you ever being ugly." He paused. "Just one more question, Jackie. Is there anything else you want to tell me?"

I shook my head.

"Let me rephrase that. Is there anything else you *should* tell me?"

"No."

"In that case, I think you're getting the high sign." Indeed, Nick was waving at me from the doorway. "And I need to mingle," Riley said.

I turned to leave.

"Jackie," he said from behind me, "I read one of your books. I liked it. But your heroine almost got killed. Not unlike you last night. I'm watching you. If I have to get you locked up for your own good I will."

I gave him a wave without turning around and added a sexy wiggle to my high-heeled walk. I could have sworn I heard him sigh. Was it followed by a soft whistle?

CHAPTER SIXTEEN

"Do you believe it?" Marcia said. "Liz is barely in the ground and Dan is leaving Lexie to go to a conference."

"Where did you hear that?" I asked.

"Bill heard it from someone who heard it from someone," she replied.

I thought back to Dan's cell phone conversation. "I remember him mentioning a conference. He said he was going. It sounded as though he was making a presentation that could help his career. Maybe he had no choice."

"Everyone has a choice," Bernice said. "I'm not going to judge him, though. Sometimes there is no *good* choice."

"I bet he's going to meet up with the woman from the funeral," Marcia said.

"What did you find out about her?" Linda asked.

"She works for Dan's company. She's an account executive based in the Washington, DC area. The men she was with were with the company also. Her name's Annalise Weiss."

"Dan looked surprised when he saw her at the funeral," Linda offered.

"Shocked is more like it," I said. "He seemed to be trying to stay away from her." I remembered seeing him shake off her hand.

"I'll bet you anything she's his current squeeze," Marcia said. She rubbed her hands together. "What do we do now?"

"Do?" I asked stupidly. "What do you mean do?" I looked around the room to see three eager pairs of eyes staring at me.

"Oh, no," I said. "There's nothing *we* need to do. Riley Furman had her in his crosshairs at the funeral. I'd be willing to bet they've already had a chat."

Marcia pouted. "Aren't you curious about her? I mean, maybe she's going to be Lexie's stepmother. We owe it to Lexie to check her out."
I closed my eyes and counted to ten. "No, we don't." When I opened my eyes my friends were looking at me speculatively. "You do remember Adam Wright tried to kill me, don't you? I am done with poking my nose in where it doesn't belong."
"Marcia has a point," Bernice said, ignoring every word I had just said. "Besides, as women we might think of ways of getting her to talk that he wouldn't." She sat straighter in her chair. "You know, *she* could be the murderer. Think about it. If Liz were out of the way, Annalise could be well on her way to being the next Mrs. Williams. It isn't a long drive from Washington to Summer Hill. She easily could have known about Dan's Memorial Day plans and taken advantage of the fireworks to go to the house and kill Liz."
"Maybe she didn't mean to kill her," Linda chipped in. "Maybe she went to the house just to talk to Liz and things got out of control. Remember the wine and the glasses. It looked like Liz was expecting someone."
"Oh, for Pete's sake," I exploded. "What was she going to do? Walk in and say "Hi, I'm Dan's mistress. I really want you to get this divorce over and let me have him?" I snorted.
"It does sound far fetched when you put it that way," Linda admitted.
"Far fetched? It sounds ridiculous!"
"Maybe she's not the killer but she knows who is," Marcia contributed.
"What about this for an idea?" Bernice asked. "She and Dan committed the murder together."
These speculations were getting crazier and crazier. I had to put a stop to it.
"Here's an idea. She's a perfectly nice woman who's in love with Dan and had nothing to do with anything."
My friends looked deflated.
"Where's the conference?" Marcia asked.

"It should be easy enough to find out," Linda replied, pulling out her tablet computer. "Let me put in the company name and see if we can find information on company events." She scrolled on the computer for a few minutes while the rest of us sat in silence. I was hoping she would find nothing and this conversation would be closed. In fact, I prayed that would be the case.

"Here it is!"

What do they say about unanswered prayers?

"There's a three-day conference at the Chesapeake Bay Marina and Spa starting tomorrow. That's near St. Mary's. It's not far."

"So what?" I asked, dreading the response.

Marcia, Bernice and Linda huddled together. "Here's the website for the resort," Linda said.

"Wow! That's gorgeous," Marcia said.

Bernice had taken over, moving through pictures on the screen. "Look at the spa! It looks so restful." Reluctantly I joined them. The picture showed a room decorated in pale blues and cream. The center room featured a reception desk and comfortable looking seating. Doors off the main area led to smaller treatment rooms decorated in the same colors, along with a hair and nail salon, steam shower and sauna. A room between the shower and sauna featured several sculpted chaises made out of mosaic tile. They faced an expanse of glass that allowed a spectacular view of the bay and a marina studded with power and sailboats.

"Those couches look like the ones on cruise ships," Bernice said. "You can shower and rest, then take a sauna and come back. They're wonderful."

"Look at their list of treatments," Linda said. "That farm to body scrub looks interesting."

Farm to body? Was that like farm to table? It sounded like you were being prepared to be that night's main course.

"I could use a massage," Bernice said, stretching like a cat.

"The inn is spectacular," Marcia said. The main building was a pale yellow structure with bright white trim built in the shape of the letter U. Outside stone pillars held up a large portico. Inside photos showcased a matching stone fireplace with wingback chairs arranged in front of it. There were inside and outside bars and restaurants and a swimming pool featuring a lazy river and a swim up bar.

"The restaurant menu looks really good," Linda said. "All locally sourced ingredients. Man, there's nothing like a crab just fished out of the bay."

Bernice scrolled some more. "Here we are. Let's see. They have a two bedroom suite on the second floor with a view of the bay. It looks really nice. Hmmm." She clicked on a tab. "Oh!" she said in surprise. "That's not bad, particularly if we split it four ways." She clicked again. "Yes, it's available."

What?

"You know what this means?" Linda said expectantly. Two eager faces turned toward her. My own was buried in my hands. "Road trip!" My friends gave each other high fives. I moaned.

"But first," Marcia squealed. "We go shopping!"

Oh, no. No, no, no. Not again. No.

Again I stood in a store with my friends, this one specializing in resort and cruise wear. Linda twirled, showing off bright Capri slacks in a paisley pattern and a thigh length tunic. "What do you think?" I had to admit that the color complimented her gray hair to flattering effect and the outfit fit perfectly, showing off her curves in a subtle fashion.

Bernice had loaded up on clothes featuring lime greens, oranges and yellow. Marcia was working her way through a large selection of tops. I had nothing, although a sleeveless floral dress with a V neck, ruffle at the waist and flowing skirt seemed to have my name on it. I sighed. At this rate Nick wouldn't get his car and I wouldn't meet my book deadline. I had worked on it only sporadically since Liz's murder.

"All right," Linda said as we carried our purchases out of the store, "Here's the plan. I'll drive. We'll meet at my house at 8:00. I figure it will take about three hours to reach the resort."

"Nick will stay at our house," Bernice said. "Maggie can come too, so you won't have anything to worry about."

Really? Why did I doubt that statement? As I drove home I considered calling Riley Furman to let him know where we were going. I decided against it. Hopefully this would turn into a pleasant girls' weekend and my friends would give up any plans of tracking down Annalise and Dan. Of course, pigs could also fly over the Chesapeake Bay.

Linda's Lexus hummed northward on Route 301, heading from Virginia into Maryland. Marcia and I sat in the back seat, perusing the spa offerings. I had pretty much decided on the verbena scrub and a manicure when Bernice spoke up. "All right, how are we going to go about finding out what Dan and this Annalise person have been up to?"

That one question burst my bubble. "If anything," I muttered.

"Oh, something's been up," Marcia said, raising her finger suggestively. We had to laugh.

"At a typical corporate meeting all the events will be published where anyone can see them," Linda explained to us corporate neophytes. "We can review these and figure out what ones might be easier to infiltrate."

Infiltrate?

"The hardest ones are likely to be the sit-down meals," she said, "followed by any corporate presentations. I was at a hotel one time where two rival firms had booked conferences at the same time. The resort never should have allowed that to happen. One of the companies actually hired security personnel to make sure no one from the other company got anywhere near its space. Our best bet will be to look for periods of spare time, followed by outside events like cocktail parties."

"Annalise will recognize you, Marcia," Bernice noted. "So you're going to need to be very careful."

Marcia tossed her magenta streaked hair and ran her hand over her short shocking pink top. "I don't look anything like I did at the funeral," she said with satisfaction.

"No, but you're hard to miss and Dan knows you," I said.

She frowned. "That's true. That's why I brought this." She pulled a curly shoulder length wig out of her capacious tote bag. "And these." She put on a pair of dark glasses. "What do you think?"

Linda looked in the rearview mirror and snorted. "I think with a little padding you'd look like a Dolly Parton impersonator."
"Well," Marcia said cheerfully, "Dan doesn't know *her.*"
"We're all going to have to be careful not to let Dan see us," I said. "I can't imagine how we'd explain our suddenly popping up at the same venue as his conference."
Bernice nodded. "I agree. I'm hoping we can catch him and Annalise together and then get her away from Dan for a friendly girls' chat."
I blew air into my bangs. "Don't count on it," I said. "I have a bad feeling about this."
"Don't be a party pooper," Marcia said. "In any event, even if we're not successful think about all the fun we're going to have."
We glided to a stop under the inn's portico. Marcia scurried out of the car before the bellhop could offer her assistance and positioned herself behind a pillar. Bernice, on the other hand, extended her hand and smiled graciously as he helped her stand. She sucked in her cheekbones and, using her runway model walk, headed toward the registration desk. Linda followed, showing a lot of trim thigh accentuated by platform wedge sandals. I watched for a moment, perplexed. If we were supposed to be inconspicuous, they were certainly doing a bad job of it. When it was my time to leave the vehicle, I gave the valet what I hoped was a 1000-watt Hollywood type style. As I entered the lobby Marcia scooted in after me. She crouched behind a potted palm, surveying the area through its leaves. Oh, boy. Mata Hari she was not.
"Ms. Bradley," a wide-eyed young woman at the desk said, "We are so thrilled to have you here." She lowered her voice. "You are even more beautiful than your pictures. I read your interview with Oprah. It was so interesting. I'm so impressed with the work you and your husband are doing."
Bernice smiled and rested her hand on top of the young woman's. "My friends and I are happy to be here." She leaned toward her. "We're looking forward to a couple days of rest. We would really, really appreciate it if your staff helped us keep a

low profile. I don't mean to be rude, but we prefer not to be inundated with people seeking autographs or pictures."

The young woman nodded. "I completely understand. Your suite has a very private entrance and it's far away from any of our conference guests. You can even dine on your porch if you like."

Bernice nodded. "Thank you. I appreciate your taking care of us. Now, if someone will show us the way to our suite?"

By now Marcia had tucked herself behind a metal sculpture of water birds taking wing.

"Right away," the woman said, handing Bernice our keys. "If we can do anything to make your stay more pleasant, let us know."

The suite did indeed seem isolated. It was on the opposite end of the building from where the conference was taking place at the end of one wing. We walked into an enormous living room with a dining area that could easily sit eight people. The couches and chairs were covered with off white fabric, accented with a variety of throw pillows in maritime hues of blue and aqua. A rug in the same colors contrasted with oak floors polished to a high sheen. Glass doors opened onto a semicircular covered porch that featured several padded chaise lounges and a rectangular dining table with seating. On either side of the living area were double doors leading to bedrooms with en suite bathrooms. Each room held two queen size beds. The baths were completely tiled and each featured a large stand-alone soaking tub.

"I'll need a ladder to get into this thing," Marcia commented, running her hand over the rim of a tub.

"I love this brand of toiletries." Linda opened a bottle and inhaled deeply.

"How much did you say this place costs?" I asked.

Bernice waved her hand in a shooing gesture. "We can afford it. Besides, I told them I'd endorse the resort if we had a good experience. They gave us a discount." I guess our friend's fame was still very much alive and well in spite of her change of profession.

"What interview with Oprah?" I asked.

Linda sighed. "Jackie, you really do need to get out more."

"It was a few months ago," Bernice said. "We were talking about the work Ray and I have been doing with our literacy foundation." She grinned and clapped her hands joyfully. "You should see the donations we've received since that interview. We're at the point where we can hire a director and a part time grant writer." Bernice did a little dance. "We're so excited. Can you imagine the people we'll be able to reach?"

We all applauded and had a group hug.

"Whatever we can do to help, we're here," we promised.

"There's a mini bar," Linda said. "There's also already a full ice bucket and a bottle of champagne." She turned to the coffee table. "Oh, look at those beautiful canapés. I think I'm going to like it here."

Marcia dropped her tote bag next to the couch and started to rummage in it. "That's all well and good," she said, "but don't forget what we're here for." She pulled out a pair of binoculars and her camera fitted with a zoom lens. She strolled onto the porch and pointed the binoculars at the opposite end of the hotel. "Good. It looks like the people at the conference are having a cocktail party on the porch downstairs." She fiddled with the setting on the glasses. While she did that Linda poured each of us a glass of champagne. Marcia sighted through the camera's viewfinder and clicked the button. She put down the camera, took a glass of champagne and raised it high. "Toast!" She said. "We are in the perfect location to see everything we need to see. This mission is good to go!"

We clinked our glasses. We were in a beautiful resort on one of the most spectacular bodies of water in the country. We were four friends united in a righteous cause. What could possibly go wrong?

CHAPTER SEVENTEEN

That evening we took Linda's advice and dressed more conservatively in order to reconnoiter the conference area. Marcia had once again changed hair color back to her natural shade. After watching this transformation, I finally realized that she was using some kind of product that easily washed out. Sometimes I'm a little slow on the uptake, particularly when it comes to fashion. The realization made me wonder if I should get a little more adventurous. After all, I had tried spandex. Of course Marcia agreed. She looked me over critically. "I think some pink highlights could be cute on you," she said, pulling out bottles of color.

"Not now!" I protested, backing away and almost falling onto the bed. "Maybe after we get back home. We're trying to be less conspicuous, not more, remember?" She reluctantly put away her supplies but I could tell from the gleam in her eye that this conversation was far from over.

The four of us made our way to the wing of the inn where the conference was being held. "See?" Linda said, waving her hand at computer monitors hanging from the ceiling. "There's today's schedule. We've already seen the cocktail party. Next they're having a buffet dinner on the grounds."

"That sounds nice," Bernice said. "It's a beautiful evening."

We looked further down the display. "Tomorrow morning there's a buffet breakfast followed by a general session," Linda continued. "It looks like after that they break into smaller groups. There's a buffet lunch followed by more sessions. They have free time after 3:00."

"What's with all the buffets?" Marcia asked.

"It's a less expensive way to feed a crowd," Linda replied. "You don't have nearly the number of wait staff you would otherwise and often the food is simpler and less expensive."

"The next day looks like more of the same," I said. "Oh, look, Dan's the keynote speaker in the morning. Then there are more sessions, blah, blah, blah, followed by a sit down dinner and a party."

"And on Sunday there's another breakfast buffet, a general session and then they leave," Bernice contributed.

"How are we going to crash this thing?" Marcia asked.

"Crash it?" I whipped my head around. "Why would we do that?"

"Isn't that the best way to see what's going on between Dan and Annalise?"

"I don't think so," Linda said. "It seems to me they'd be more likely to be together during the free time tomorrow afternoon."

"I think we need a back up plan," Marcia insisted. "Just in case we do want to get in, how do we do it?" She glanced at the few people still in the reception area. "Everyone has an ID badge."

We walked further into the hall and spotted a desk stacked with brochures. "I have an idea." Linda strolled casually over and came back grinning. "There are some name badges that haven't been picked up."

"So what?" I asked, dreading the answer.

"We take one."

"Say what?" Bernice said.

Linda sighed as though we were exceptionally slow students. "We take a badge that no one uses. One of us impersonates that person and in she goes."

"Wait a minute," I said, starting to panic. "What if that person shows up?"

"We wait until tomorrow. There will surely be some people who arrive late this evening or tomorrow morning. The general session in the morning will probably be our best opportunity to grab a badge. In my experience those are key events an attendee wouldn't want to miss, so everyone will be checked in by then. There are always a few people who, for one reason or other, can't attend even though they planned to. We just have to wait for the people manning the table to leave."

"What if you need some identification?" I asked, my panic rising.
"Then you say you left everything in your room and walk away."
Easy enough. Maybe.
"Some companies have become more sophisticated," Linda continued, casually picking up a badge. "They use face scans or fingerprints to activate a badge. More often than not that happens at conferences where people earn continuing education credits. From the schedule this looks more like an awards meeting." She fingered the badge and put it back on the table. "These look like very simple name badges. I think we're in the clear where security is concerned."
Oh, good.
"What if you run into someone who knows the person the badge belongs to?" Bernice asked. I had a feeling she was as nervous as I was.
"You say, 'oh, my goodness, they gave me the wrong badge." Marcia said. "Then you turn and leave the room."
"So who is the lucky person to do the crashing if it comes to that?" I asked.
We scrutinized each other.
"Not me," Bernice said, holding up her hands and backing away.
"I have to agree," I said reluctantly. "Your face is too well known, particularly after that entrance today." I was hit by an unpleasant thought. "Did you do that on purpose?"
Bernice shook her head vehemently. "My public persona got us the suite. And the discount. That's all."
"I'll do it!" Marcia said.
The rest of us considered this option for about half a second.
"No," I said.
"No offense, Sweetie," Bernice said, trying to soften my reply, "but we know you too well. There's no way you could blend into a corporate crowd."
As a person Bernice, Marcia and I turned to Linda.
"You talk corporate speak," Marcia said. "You would just fade into the crowd."
Linda considered her suggestion. "Maybe," she said, "but I think

Jackie should do it."

What? Why me? There was no way I was doing this. I crossed my arms and stared back at my friends. No, no, no. This time I was standing my ground.

"You think fast on your feet. Also, you are better than I am at getting people to open up to you." She paused. "You also run faster."

That was not something I needed to hear.

The room felt as though it was tilting. "I'll tell you what," I said. "*If*, and that's a very big if, one of us goes in, we'll flip a coin."

Linda smiled so widely that her teeth sparkled in the light of the corridor. She reminded me of a shark. "Deal," she said.

"I get to choose the coin," I said.

Her face fell. Just as I suspected, she must have had some trick coin that would let her win the toss no matter what. Shame on her. "Why would you bring some fancy coin with you?" I asked. I looked around at the group. "Were you planning something like this?"

Linda smiled. "I wouldn't say planning, but it never hurts to be prepared."

Oh, good grief.

"I don't know about you," Bernice said, "but I'm hungry. I could really go for a glass of wine or two and some fresh seafood. The restaurant menu looks fantastic."

"Let's see if the outside restaurant is open," Marcia suggested. "It might be part of the conference venue tonight. If it is we'll have to go somewhere else."

Indeed it was closed. We opted to eat on our balcony, which very conveniently overlooked the area where the conferees were eating dinner.

"This is the life," Marcia sighed, leaning back in her chair. Our waiter popped the cork from a bottle of wine and offered the contents for tasting. Bernice rolled the wine around in her mouth before nodding that it should be poured.

"I miss Ray," Bernice said. She took a sip of her wine. "I mean, I love spending time with you, but this place is so romantic."

Marcia nodded enthusiastically. "Just think about the bathtub

alone. Last year Bob and I went to an amazing resort in the Poconos. It had one of those really deep tubs and we…"
"Stop already." I said. To my surprise my voice quivered.
Linda reached out to hold my hand.
"I miss Lars," I whispered. "I really, really miss him."
"We know, honey." Marcia covered my other hand. "I'm sorry."
I shook my head impatiently and took a deep sip of wine. "I'm OK," I said. Bernice blew me a kiss across the table.
The waiter returned with plates of salads crowned with farm fresh vegetables and a basket of piping hot rolls.
"Who needs an entrée?" Linda groaned, slathering honey butter onto a hunk of bread.
The sun sank slowly over the bay, turning both the water and sky orange and crimson. Masts of sailboats were silhouetted against the darkening sky. In the distance a water bird gave a lonely cry. It was picture perfect. Bernice was right. It also was romantic. Perhaps some day I'd have someone special enough to share the view with. It was hard to imagine, but I noted that I was beginning to contemplate life post Lars.
Our entrees arrived. I looked appreciatively at my crab cake, accompanied by asparagus and a fresh corn risotto. Maybe I should include a risotto recipe in my book? The one I had yet to write. Never mind.
After dinner we sipped chilled glasses of limoncello, drifting into a state of languor produced by alcohol and rich food. The noise decibel from the buffet below increased. Marcia picked up her binoculars. "Oh!" She leaned forward, adjusting the lenses. "I see them!"
We moved to the railing, craning our necks. Indeed, Dan and Annalise sat below us at a small table. They leaned toward each other, talking intensely. At one point she covered his hand with hers. After a moment he moved it. Her face fell. Dan hesitated, then lifted her chin and kissed her gently. They talked a while longer. He rose and caressed the top of her head, which was bent over the table. I would bet she was crying.
"Ladies," Marcia said, "I think there's trouble in Paradise."

CHAPTER EIGHTEEN

The morning dawned clear and bright. I stood on our balcony with a cup of coffee and watched the sunshine sparkle off the bay. The ripples on the water's surface were luminescent, shimmering with shades of silver and green.

"Beautiful, isn't it?" Linda leaned on the railing and inhaled deeply.

I agreed.

"Bernice suggested that we go for a boat ride this morning. Everyone at the conference should be in meetings until three or so. Let's consider this free time just for us."

"Sounds good." I said.

"There's just one thing I have to do before we go," Linda said, smiling mischievously.

Oh, no, The identification badge. She was really going to try to get one.

"I still don't see why we might want to infiltrate the conference," I said.

"We might hear some good gossip," Marcia said from behind us. She threw a leotard clad leg onto the balcony railing and bent forward to touch her toes. After staying in that position for a while she repeated the exercise with the other leg. Then she pulled one leg behind her and touched the back of her head with her toes. That also got repeated. I watched her with mild disgust. She was so fit. Well, I wasn't in terrible shape. I could probably do the front toe touch. I lifted a leg. Then I cupped my hands behind it and lifted it onto the railing, staggering as I did so.

"Easy, Tiger!" Linda laughed, holding me upright.

I bent forward. I touched my head to my knee. My hands reached my ankles. Almost. I guess it could be worse. Now, however, I had to figure out how to get both legs back on terra firma without falling over. I grabbed my leg with both hands and pulled it sideways. By now Linda and Marcia were laughing so hysterically that they were no help. I gave a little jump and my leg came back to earth.

"Maybe you should re-think joining the gym," Bernice slouched against the wall, grinning from ear to ear.

We enjoyed a continental breakfast on our balcony, watching boats pull out of their moorings and sail toward the open water of the bay. Bernice had a brochure in front of her. "There are several cruises each day," she reported. "I think we should do the one at 10:00. It goes out for an hour. Later in the day and especially on the water the sun could get too intense for us."

Linda nodded. "That sounds like fun." She consulted what looked like notes. "The conference will have a snack break at 2:00. If we're going to try to spy on Dan and his girlfriend that could be a good time to do so."

"I don't know," I protested. "We've already done some spying. They don't look like a happy couple. Why don't we just have some fun and go home? The spa here looks great and so does the pool. Also, there are a lot of interesting historical sites nearby."

"You could be right," Bernice conceded. "We know Dan and Analise have a relationship. What more do we need to know?" Level headed Bernice tended to side with me more often than Linda and, in particular, Marcia.

"Where she was on Memorial Day," Marcia said. "And maybe some of Dan's co-workers have noticed any behavior changes. For example, has he been angry? Aggressive? Sad?"

"So what?" I asked, knowing I was fighting a losing battle.

Marcia chewed a pastry thoughtfully. "Maybe we're missing something where Dan's concerned. It could be there's an entire person other than the one we think we know. That person might be able to kill his wife."

I kept my opinion that the Dan we knew was the one we'd always known to myself and stuffed a spoonful of fresh berries into my mouth.

"Let's go," Linda said once we had finished breakfast.
"Where to?" I asked.
"First you and I are going to check out the conference. Then we can head down to the pier in time to catch the boat."
"Why am I going with you to the conference?" I asked.
"You're my lookout," Linda said, looking like this was a no-brainer. I pouted all the way down the hallway and into the elevator.
"This is a truly stupid idea," I said.
"Oh, come on," Linda said, pulling me along. "You've been out-voted."
"I don't remember a vote," I grumbled.
"It was a silent one," she said.
That figures.
The conference hall indeed was fairly empty when we arrived. We could hear voices coming from a large room to our left. Two women were in the process of closing the doors. "Good! The first session has begun," Linda said. "Keep an eye out." She made her way toward the registration table.
"For what?" I asked.
"Anyone other than hotel staff," she said as she reached the table. I stood in the middle of the empty hallway as she stretched her hand toward the table. "Quick! Someone's coming!"
Two latecomers were hurrying toward the conference room doors. Linda stuffed something in her pocket. She pretended to be studying the monitors as the conference goers passed her. I grabbed a used newspaper and ducked my head. They entered the closed off room.
"Let's go," Linda hissed.
We scurried down the hall and into the main reception area. "Here's what I got," Linda said, holding out her hand. In it was a badge reading 'Rachel Johnson, Columbia, South Carolina.'
"Who in the world is Rachel Johnson?" I asked.
Linda shrugged as she pressed the bell for the elevator. "I don't know. It doesn't matter. You can make it up as you go along."
"Me?" I put my hands on my hips. "What do you mean, me? I

thought we were going to flip a coin."

"We voted."

"How can you vote when I'm not there?" I was trotting along beside her as we returned to our room to grab our sun gear.

"Three's a quorum."

"Says who?" I demanded. I started flapping my arms up and down. "Three's a disaster, that's what three is! I am *not* doing this."

Linda glanced at me as she unlocked the door. "You look ridiculous."

"Yeah, well just wait until this afternoon. I am *not,* I repeat *not* going."

The four of us squabbled all the way to the boat deck. I decided to remain in a huffy mood and sat away from my so-called friends in the bow of the boat. It didn't take long, however, for the rhythm of the gentle waves and the beating of the sun to begin to mellow my mood. The captain slowed as we passed a school of snowy egrets standing in shallow water, lifting their backward jointed knees high as they searched for small fish and other tasty morsels in the shallows. He gave a fascinating talk about the history of the bay, not sugar coating the environmental challenges it faced, and emphasizing the improvements in water quality that had resulted from the hard work of many dedicated groups. I decided I had enjoyed enough direct sunlight and joined the rest of the group for the return trip.

"Are you mad at us?" Marcia asked with concern

I sighed. It was so hard to stay angry with this group. "No, but I still don't see the point of my going to this snack thing, other than to possibly get something good to eat. What am I going to say to people? What if they ask me about Columbia South Carolina? I've never been there in my life. I can't talk about the company's products. I don't even understand what they are. Can't you see what a truly terrible idea this is?"

"Just try to listen and watch for Dan and Annalise. If someone really pushes you, claim you have an appointment and leave."

"Or just run to the restroom," Marcia suggested. "That's a real conversation buster."

Now there was sage advice.

"Dan is going to see me."

"He won't recognize you by the time we're done with you," Marcia promised.

I gulped.

That afternoon I sat patiently in our suite, allowing Bernice to work her model quality makeup magic on me. "You're looking good," she assured me. "Really professional with just enough makeup." She sat back and admired her handiwork. "Jackie, why don't you do this more often? Wait 'til you see how beautiful you look."

I couldn't decide if that was a compliment or an insult.

"Now put this on," Marcia instructed, pulling another wig out of her bag. This one had straight hair in a strawberry blonde color. I pulled it on and she tugged until she had it the way she wanted it. Immediately my head began to itch. I started to scratch. Marcia swatted my hand. "Don't do that!" I put my hands in my lap.

"Now, wear these." She took out a pair of eyeglasses with clear lenses.

"What did you do? Buy out a costume store?"

"Just about," Marcia laughed.

"Now look at yourself, Jackie," Bernice instructed. "The only way Dan would recognize you would be if you got up close to him." She narrowed her eyes at me. "And you're not going to do that, right?"

"Right," I said. I hoped. I studied my reflection in the mirror in astonishment. Bernice was right. I looked like a totally different person. The makeup was professional but understated. The wig color went well with my skin tone and the glasses were actually flattering. I turned my head this way and that. Maybe I'd ask Bernice to give me some makeup lessons. And maybe I should go for glasses instead of contact lenses. I felt like a new me.

"Columbia South Carolina is the capitol of South Carolina," Linda read from her tablet. "It is a city of about 135,000, home to the University of South Carolina, whose football team is the Gamecocks. It sits at the convergence of three rivers…"

"Stop!" I put my hands over my ears. "That is information overload. If anyone asks me I'll just smile and say it's a wonderful city."

Linda shut her tablet. "That'll work."

I made my way to the conference center, where a couple hundred people were milling about. Some glanced at my name tag. Most just said hello and moved toward the snack tables. I helped myself to a cookie and nibbled it, moving slowly around the area.

"Hi, I'm Julie!" A bubbly blonde held out her hand. I gave her mine.

"Rachel."

"You're from South Carolina," she said, looking at my nametag. "I've been to Charleston but I've never been to Columbia."

"They're very different cities," I said, winging it.

"Of course. There's nothing like Charleston," Julie said. She was right about that. The glorious antebellum city had long been a favorite of mine for long weekend getaways. The beautiful shotgun houses with their lush cloistered gardens enchanted me, as did the mansions along the Battery and the splendid views of Fort Sumter. And the food! Lars and I had talked about buying a second home near Charleston but came away with a bad case of sticker shock. Julie was right though. Charleston was unique. Columbia was, I was sure, delightful, but I doubted it could hold a candle to its sister city.

"How are you enjoying the conference?" Julie asked.

"It's interesting," I said.

"What sessions did you go to today?"

I managed to take a bite of cookie and indicated I had a full mouth.

She waved a hand. "Same old, same old. Some were good, others…" She rolled her eyes.

I nodded in agreement and took another bite.

"I'm really looking forward to Dan Williams' talk tomorrow, aren't you?"

"I sure am," I said. I edged toward the table and grabbed a

brownie.

"I can't imagine what he's going through," Julie said, her eyes huge.

"Do you know him?" I asked.

She nodded enthusiastically. "We're in the same district so I see him fairly frequently." She lost some of her sparkle. "I can't believe what happened to his wife. Poor Dan. Can you imagine having your wife murdered? And now the cops have been crawling all over the place. They've interviewed us co-workers and his boss more than once."

"They have?" I didn't have to fake being interested.

"Oh, yes," Julie whispered. "They found out he's been seeing someone. Apparently, they've been questioning both of them."

"You don't think Dan had anything to do with it, do you?" I asked, pretending to be fascinated.

Julie shook her head. "I don't. But he's certainly changed in the past six months. If I were Annalise, I'd be rethinking that relationship. He's been so moody. I guess he's the same as ever with his clients, but at the office he's either yelling or depressed. He scares me a little. And one time Annalise had a bruise on her arm. She swears it was from her dog jumping on her, but I'm not so sure."

Now that was interesting.

Julie leaned forward conspiratorially. "They were supposed to get together that weekend, but something happened to change that. I know she went down to see him, but she told me things didn't work out. She was really upset." She looked at her watch. "Oops! I signed up for a yoga class at three. Nice talking to you."

She trotted away. I swallowed the last bit of brownie and decided I'd heard enough.

The ladies were waiting in the suite for me. I reported back.

"I just saw Dan and three other guys take off for the golf course," Bernice said, gesturing over the balcony.

"In that case, I have a farm to body wrap appointment," Linda announced.

"Hot stone massage for me," Bernice said.

"Mud wrap for me," Marcia announced.

They left together. Little rascals. I hadn't scheduled anything. I decided to head to those wonderful mosaic benches in the spa and edit the book whose first run I had recently finished.

Half an hour later I was snuggled in a light cotton robe, had a glass of orange flavored water at my elbow and was settling down for an editing session. The creative juices were beginning to flow when someone eased onto the bench next to me.

I glanced over briefly, and then looked again. The woman next to me had white blonde hair, sculpted cheekbones and a body to die for. Very casually I knocked my glass to the ground, spilling some of the water on her.

"I'm so sorry!" I cried. I tossed my legs over the side of the bench and reached for my glass.

The woman turned to me and offered a tremulous smile. I looked into the eyes of Annalise Weiss. She'd clearly been crying. I decided to offer some comfort and see what I could learn from Dan Williams' girlfriend. Never mind that my conscience was reminding me to be nice. Maybe I'd listen to it. Maybe not.

CHAPTER NINETEEN

I peered sympathetically at Annalise. "You look like you've had a bad day."

Once again she tried to smile. "Sometimes things don't go like you expect."

"That sounds like the story of my life," I said.

A spa attendant replaced my glass of fruited water and placed one on the table next to Annalise.

"Really?" She asked.

'You don't know the half of it' I thought. Out loud I said, "Any time you have a teenager, a nutty puppy and a cranky , things can get pretty crazy in a hurry. Oh, and don't forget the squash bugs. Fighting them is constant chaos."

She ventured a laugh. "Squash bugs. At least they're not one of my problems." She gestured toward the pile of papers lying in my lap, covered with red squiggles. "That looks like a lot of work. What do you do?"

"I'm a writer," I replied.

"That's so interesting. I love to read. What kinds of things do you write?"

"I'm a mystery writer."

Annalise sat up a little straighter. "Mysteries are some of my favorites. I wonder if I've read anything you've written. What's your name?"

"Jackie Olsen," I said, wondering whether I should have used a pseudonym.

"This is so exciting!" Annalise said. "I've read every book in your series featuring the librarian. I've really enjoyed them."

I managed a genuine smile. "I'm so glad to hear that."

Annalise narrowed her eyes at me. "Wait a minute. Your name is familiar for another reason. Let me think…" She sat up straight and glared at me accusingly. "Dan Williams has a neighbor by that name. Is that you?"

Busted.

I decided to be honest. "It is indeed." I tried a chuckle. "Strange coincidence, isn't it?"

"I'm not so sure." Annalise took a deep swallow from her water. "I don't believe in coincidences."

Silence hung between us. Finally, she let out a huge sigh. "You're not going to tell me the real reason you're here, are you?"

"I'm on a girl's weekend with some friends," I said, honestly enough. "They're all getting fancy spa treatments and I decided to get some work done."

Annalise shook her head. "I don't buy it. Dan told me that you were going to try to help him clear his name. Is that why you're here? But why would you be following Dan? That doesn't make a lot of sense."

No kidding. And when did Dan turn into such a blabbermouth anyway?

She gasped. "I know! You have me pegged as the other woman! You think I have something to do with his wife's death. I'm the evil home wrecker out to snag a rich husband." She stood and tightened the belt on her robe. "Well, you have it all wrong!" She turned to leave.

"Annalise," I said, "As hard as it is to believe, I have no preconceived notions where you're concerned. I saw you with Dan at Liz's funeral. I've seen you here at the conference with him. It looks to me like you're more than friends, but I'm willing to be proven wrong."

Her shoulders sagged. "You're not wrong on the last point. At least, you weren't. At this point I don't know what Dan and I are." The tears reappeared.

I took pity on her. "Why don't we get a drink?" I proposed. "It has to be five o'clock somewhere."

"It's after that here," Annalise pointed out. She thought a moment. "I guess we can do that. I don't know what good it will do.

Why don't we meet in the corner bar in half an hour?"

"We can do that," I said, "or you can come to our suite if you prefer."

She raised an eyebrow. "A suite, huh? Nice way to travel. But no thank you. If we meet in the bar I can walk out whenever I want."

What did she think we were going to do? Hogtie her and shoot her up with truth serum?

"Corner bar it is," I said, rising and gathering my papers. "You need to know that my friends will be there with me, just in case that makes you uncomfortable."

"I haven't been comfortable since Dan's wife died," Annalise said, heading toward the exit.

Almost every head turned when Annalise entered the bar. She wore a white strapless sundress with a fitted bodice and a flared skirt that stopped just below the knee. An intricate string of silver and turquoise beads circled her neck and turquoise earrings hung from her lobes. She had allowed her hair to fall in soft waves to her shoulders. Her makeup was subtle and flawless. She looked like a young Grace Kelly.

"Wow," Marcia whispered. "No wonder Dan fell for her."

We had decided to have dinner at a seafood restaurant in town and I had worn my new flirty sundress in honor of the occasion. I had felt bright and shiny when I put it on. Now I felt dowdy compared to the glowing Annalise Weiss. Even Bernice's beauty was subdued compared to hers.

Annalise approached us with the grace of a princess and sank into a chair next to mine. I performed the introductions and we ordered our beverages. Annalise ordered a craft beer and drank it out of the bottle. She was quite a contradiction I thought, comparing the sophisticated exterior to the girl next door behavior.

"So you all live on the same street as Dan?" Annalise asked. She seemed amused.

We agreed that we did, indeed, live on the street.

"What do you want of me?" she asked.

Bernice, Linda and I exchanged glances. It seemed that I was to take the lead. "How long have you known Dan?" I asked.

She thought for a moment. “About two years, I guess. That’s when I was transferred to the Washington DC territory office. Dan was assigned as my manager and we got to know each other quite well.”

“I’ll bet,” Marcia muttered. Uh oh. I had a bad feeling Ms. Tact was about to take over.

“I heard that,” Annalise said, still looking amused.

“Well then,” Marcia began, leaning forward. “How long…” Linda kicked her ankle. “Ow!”

“I already told Jackie,” Annalise said, taking a sip of her beer, “I am not an evil marriage buster.”

“How would *you* describe your relationship with Dan?”

Annalise’s eyes clouded up again. “I thought we were in love,” she said.

“You chose a difficult road, falling for a married man,” Bernice said levelly.

It was Annalise’s turn to lean forward in her chair. “Dan and I started going out about four months ago. He’d already been separated for two months. His marriage was over. We’d always been attracted to each other, but we never did anything or even said anything inappropriate until he left his wife. You can’t blame me for his marriage falling apart.” She started to leave.

“Wait,” Linda put a hand on her arm. “So you thought you were in love. Why don’t you think it now? That sounds like a pretty miserable place to be.” Thank goodness for Linda’s ability to deal with people when they were upset.

Annalise sat back down and picked at the label on her bottle. “He’s just been so weird. One moment he’s like normal, the next he’s flying off the handle, and then I caught him crying in the shower. Now he says he just wants time before he’s with me. He won’t talk about it. Sometimes he can barely look at me. At the funeral he wouldn’t have anything to do with me.”

“Can you blame him?” Bernice said. “Look, I’m going to tell you some things I’m sure you don’t want to hear. Whether or not Dan was separated from Liz, he was still married to her. You let yourself be put in the middle of a sticky situation. For all you know they could have changed their minds about divorcing." Annalise shook her head. "Hear me out." Bernice persisted. "They were married for over twenty years. Most of those years were happy. Of course he's crying in the shower. Even if he didn't love her at the end, he did love her for a long, long time. If you stay together you are going to have to deal with those memories."

"But she was so mean to him," Annalise whispered.

"Yes, she was," I agreed. "But that was very recent. Now that he knows that in all likelihood Liz changed because she was sick, Dan will probably have a lot of guilt and regret to deal with."

Marcia took a sip of her cosmopolitan. "Do you have any children?" Annalise shook her head. She appeared to be about ten years younger than we were, so any children would have been small. Marcia made a sweeping gesture. "Well, we do."

Linda raised her hand. "I'm an aunt," she said. "My nieces are like daughters to me. There's nothing I wouldn't do for them. So I feel like I have children."

"That's something else you and Dan will have to figure out. Where does Lexie fit into the scheme of things?" I put in. "Not only was he a married man, but he's a father, and he's a good father."

"I know that," Annalise said. "I was hoping Lexie and I could be friends."

"Maybe at some time," I said. "And maybe it would be easier if Liz hadn't died. I suspect it's going to take a long time before Lexie even wants to hear about you. It may take weeks, it may take months, it may take years. I guarantee you that Dan will make her his first priority. You're going to have to wait or you need to be prepared to let him go."

"I wanted Liz to just let the divorce go through, but every time it looked they were making progress she would come back with some other outrageous demand," Annalise said, gesturing for another beer. "She kept twisting the screws tighter and tighter. It was as though she didn't really want to let him go but she didn't want him back either. And she kept playing games with visitation. That broke his heart. I thought we could be happy. I know how much he loves his daughter. I'm glad he does. As far as I'm concerned, that makes him a better man. And it gives me faith that he'll be a good father if we ever have children. And yes, before you ask, I know how old he is. I don't think it's too late to have a family when you're in your forties. Lots of people do it, and do it well. I thought we could be happy and Lexie could be happy with us." She sipped her drink.

"Did you do anything to try to make Liz give in?" Linda asked.

Annalise shook her head. "I tried, but I changed my mind."

"What do you mean?" Bernice asked.

"I went to talk to her, but I chickened out."

"When was this?" I asked.

"Memorial Day weekend," Annalise replied. "I knew Dan was going to be in Summer Hill with his family. He was staying at his parents' house because his landlord was having some renovations done to his building and the noise and the dust were making him crazy. He didn't want me to go with him. He hadn't told anyone he was seeing me." For the first time she looked as though a light bulb was turning on.

"Oh my God, do you think he was just leading me on? Just for the company and the...the sex? Do you think that's why he didn't tell his family about me?" She pressed a cocktail napkin to her eyes and slumped in her chair.

"Don't jump to conclusions," Linda said. "It was a difficult time and maybe he just thought the timing was bad."

"His mother's not the most welcoming woman either," I said, remembering my encounter with Adele Williams at the funeral. "She wouldn't have greeted you with open arms."

"I'll say amen to that," Marcia chipped in. Those of us who knew Adele had a chuckle at her expense.

"So what did you do about seeing Liz?" I asked.

"I drove down to Summer Hill and checked into a hotel. I knew where Liz lived. Dan had mentioned she always had a big party on Memorial Day. I thought maybe she'd be in a good mood and that I might be able to talk to her after the party."

"And so?"

She lifted her chin defiantly. "I drove to her house to confront her."

"About what time was that?" Bernice asked.

"I guess it was around 7 or 7:30. It was shortly before the fireworks began. It was pretty quiet at her house when I got there."

"Did you go in?" Marcia asked.

By now we had forgotten our drinks and were leaning toward Annalise to make sure we heard every word.

"Do you mean did I go in and stab her to death?" Annalise asked defiantly.

"Well, when you put it that way," Marcia began. She swung toward Linda. "Would you stop kicking me?" Linda just rolled her eyes.

"No, I didn't go in," Annalise said.

"Did you run out of courage?" Linda asked sympathetically.

"No," Annalise shook her head. "When I pulled up to her house I saw another car in front of the house." She paused and looked around dramatically, almost as though she were telling a story. "It took me a minute, but I recognized the car." She took a deep breath. "It was Dan's."

I don't think anything could have shocked us more. Linda took a big gulp of her Manhattan. I slugged down my remaining chardonnay and held up a hand for a refill. Bernice and Marcia sat in stunned silence.

"Did you see Dan?" Bernice asked.

"No. I didn't stick around. I drove back to the hotel, checked out, came home and cried myself to sleep. But here's the strange part. Dan swears he wasn't there. I've begged him to tell me the truth, but he keeps saying the same thing. He never went to Liz's house that night." The tears were falling down her beautiful cheeks. "Don't you see?" She sobbed. "After that and with the way he's been acting, I'm afraid." She reached out for a hand to hold and grabbed Bernice's. "I'm afraid he killed Liz."

CHAPTER TWENTY

Our dinner that evening was more subdued than it otherwise would have been. We sat outside in a beautiful bay breeze and ate fabulous fresh seafood. We drank fruity cocktails and crisp wine. We talked about anything other than Dan and Liz, but they weren't far from our minds.

The following morning, I decided that I wanted to hear Dan's speech. I donned my 'Rachel' disguise and sauntered into the conference hall. Annalise squinted at me from a distance. Deciding she recognized me she walked up and stood at my side. "Who are you supposed to be?" she asked. Then she turned and looked at my nametag. "Rachel Johnson," she read. She stifled a giggled. "I have to tell you that you don't look anything like her."

"No? Not even close?" I asked.

She snorted. "Not even close." I thought she was going to fall into hysterical laughter. "To begin with," she said, "She's African-American."

Oh snap. We never thought about that.

"She weighs at least two hundred pounds and she's five foot three," Annalise continued, obviously enjoying my discomfort. "And if she were here she'd be glad handing everyone in the room. A lot of people know her. You're lucky no one has focused on your name tag. You would be so busted.

"OK, time to go." I tried to leave, but Annalise pulled on my elbow. "Come on. Let's sit together. Maybe people will think we have more than one Rachel Johnson from Columbia in the company. Or maybe if you're with me they won't even look at your name tag."

I took a gulp of recirculated air and squared my shoulders. How bad could things possibly get? If I had only known. I didn't, however, so with Annalise at my side I marched into the lecture hall. Dan's presentation was good. It was very, very good. He was the weekend's motivational speaker, and he could really crank up a crowd, which surprised me. Here was a side of Dan I never knew. He received a standing ovation and afterwards people began spilling from the room.

"Have you figured out anything since we talked?" Annalise asked, smiling and waving at people as she escorted me into the central hall.

"There's something niggling at the corner of my brain," I said, "but I can't seem to pull it out. The girls and I are going to do some antiquing today and head home tomorrow. Maybe leaving here will help me clear my head."

Annalise inhaled sharply and I looked in the direction of her stare. Two suited men approached Dan. Another stood in the shadows of an alcove. Annalise and I crab crawled in their direction. As we watched, one of the men pulled back his jacket and showed Dan a gold shield.

"Oh my God," Annalise whispered, slapping her hand to her mouth.

"Mr. Williams," the man in the suit said. "We'd like you to come with us."

"Why?" I couldn't tell if Dan truly didn't know or he was trying to downplay the situation. Heads were beginning to turn.

Fortunately the man was speaking softly, apparently trying not to make a scene. "We need you to come with us for questioning with regards to the murder of your wife, Elizabeth Williams."

Dan paled and his knees seemed to sag. His head swiveled around and he locked eyes with Annalise. His eyes widened in shock as he took me in. In spite of my disguise, he immediately recognized me. "I'm innocent," he mouthed. "Help me, Jackie."

Dan nodded at the men and strode toward the conference exit.

Next to me Annalise was sagging. I put a supportive arm around her waist and began to lead her away. All around us tongues were wagging. The man in the alcove stepped into the light, gray eyes flashing.

"Help me, Jackie?" Riley Furman echoed. The cords in his neck showed tightly and he was clenching and unclenching his fists.
I wheeled on him. "Here? You had to do this here?" I was still supporting Annalise. "In the middle of this event, with all of his colleagues around him, with his giving what might have been the most important speech in his career, you had to come here?"
Furman stepped back, shocked by my reaction.
"Did you truly think he was going to run away from you? Leave the country? What made you do this?" I demanded, starting to cry angry tears. Annalise was crying along with me. "Shame on you!" I hissed. "Shame on you! To think I ever thought you were a decent man."
Riley reeled back as though I had hit him.
I shepherded Annalise out of the hall.
"Now wait a minute," the detective said, stepping into my path. "How dare you question the way I do my job?"
"You didn't have to humiliate Dan that way," I said. "That was just wrong."
"What are you doing here anyway?" Riley asked, looking me up and down and going on the attack.
Annalise, completely confused, was whipping her head between the two of us.
"I was trying to find something to help my friend," I said. "It's clear to me that you've made up your mind. You have no intention of finding out who killed Liz. You're just trying to put another notch on your gun by closing this case fast."
"I'm doing...what am I doing?" Riley asked, looking puzzled.
"You know perfectly well what I mean!" I stamped my foot.
By now we were at the elevator. Out of pure pique I tore the wig off my head and threw it at him. He caught it easily.
"Did you?" He asked.
"Did I what?"
"Did you find anything that could help Dan Williams?"
"No," I said. I hesitated. "I'm not sure."
Riley handed the wig to Annalise, who took it in shocked silence.
"Well, what is it?" he asked impatiently.

"I don't know," I admitted. I gestured toward my head. "There's something here, but I can't seem to pull it together."
Furman growled. "Well, that is truly helpful. Enough is enough. I am going to have you charged with obstruction of justice. You are going to jail. There will be no more interfering with this investigation."
"You know who my lawyer is," I spit, pushing past him. I hit the elevator button. "And since when don't you use contractions?"
"It only happens when I am well and thoroughly pissed off."
"Well good, because so am I."
"Jackie, for a smart woman you are being really stupid. You are far worse than Jessica Fletcher."
"Oh, yeah?" I said. "You are a badge flashing, career busting, overdressed conference crasher." The bell dinged and I thrust Annalise into the elevator before me.
Riley put his foot in the door. "Jackie..." he said.
I stabbed at the 'close door' button. "What?" I snapped.
He kissed me.
What?
Still holding the door open, he kissed me. I mean he really kissed me, one of those kisses that makes your body start tingling at your toes and sends flashes of light into your brain. Annalise was ogling us. I didn't know what would happen if her eyes bugged open any further.
I wish I could say I pushed him away, but I didn't. I came up for air. "You are despicable," I said, my voice cracking.
"Stay out of my investigation," he said. He removed his foot and the door slid closed.
Annalise, still holding the wig, continued to stare at me. "What was that about?" she asked.
"Darned if I know," I admitted. I pushed the button for the second floor and the shelter of my friends' love and support.
Unfortunately, I didn't get much of either.
"He did what?" Bernice gasped.
"That kiss was a doozy!" Annalise exclaimed. "The man knows what he's doing. I mean, my toes were curling and I wasn't any-

where near him."
"You're not helping," I said, glaring at her.
"Tongue and all?" Linda asked speculatively.
"Most definitely," Annalise replied.
"Jackie has a boyfriend," Marcia said in a sing song tone.
"Do not," I muttered, channeling a middle schooler denying a school yard crush.
"Oh, girlfriend," Bernice said, clapping her hands, "this is exciting!"
"Is not."
"Is so."
Marcia laughed so hard it sounded like a donkey braying. She pulled a bottle of champagne and pulled the cork. "Welcome back to life!" she said. "It's about time!"
We all sat on the balcony watching the boats move in and out of the harbor.
"Do you really think you have something that could help Dan?" Linda asked finally.
"I'm getting there," I said. "I'm getting there."
If I could just erase the memory of that kiss, it might be much easier

•

CHAPTER TWENTY ONE

The next day my friends and I were once again sitting at what I had come to think of as command central, a/k/a, my kitchen table.

"I don't know exactly what to do with this copy of Liz's journal," Bernice admitted, frowning at her papers.

I don't understand why Lexie gave it to you. What did she expect us to get out of it?" She was clearly frustrated.

"It looks like a list of all of her appointments, whether they were legitimate or she was involved in her nefarious activities," I said.

"Here," Linda passed around new copies. "I took off everything like a doctor's appointment. What we're left with should, for the most part, be outside activities, like when she was meeting with someone like Adam Wright. I know some of the initials could belong to personal friends, but it's a start."

"Liz sure was compulsive about keeping appointment records," I said, scanning the new pages.

"She had a lot going on," Bernice said. "Had to keep all her activities organized. You know, who she was blackmailing, who was selling drugs, who she was in business with."

"We get the picture," Linda said.

"There are an awful lot of the initials AW on here," Marcia said, starting to highlight the letters.

"She seems to have quite a few people with those initials in her life," Bernice mused. "What an odd coincidence. Let's see, who do we have? Adam Wright, Amanda Wilkinson..."

"Otherwise known as the gold-digging witch," Marcia muttered.

"Annalise Weiss, Aaron Winters. I guess that finishes the list."

"There's one more," I said. "Adele Williams."

"Oh, come on, Dan's mother?" Bernice said incredulously.
I shrugged. "I'm just trying to make sure we haven't missed anything."
"We've talked to everyone but Aaron Winter," Linda said. "How in the world do we tackle him?"
Marcia sat back and chewed on her pen. "You know him, Linda, since he did that legal work for the hospital. Maybe you could contact him for us."
I played my ace in the hole. "Have you checked your mailboxes today?" To a person they had not. "Well, look what came in the mail." I held up a glossy flier. "Guess who's running for office?"
"And look at that perfect family," Marcia said sarcastically.
"What would you do to keep an affair quiet if you were trying to break into politics?" I asked.
"Anything," Bernice said. "Just about anything."
"He's having a rally," Linda said, pointing at the picture of Aaron Winter's perfectly groomed head. "I think we should go." She smiled like the cat that had swallowed the canary. I just hoped that bird wouldn't give us indigestion.
"I hate politics," Bob complained, holding the door open for the rest of us as we entered the venue for Aaron Winters' rally.
"Not me," Ray enthused. "In fact, I'm thinking seriously of running for town council."
"Over my dead body," Bernice muttered, swatting her husband's arm. "Are you nuts?"
"I'd vote for you, Ray," Marcia said loyally.
"Yeah, well that's a party of one." Bernice's eyes shot her friend daggers.
"I'm with Ray," I found myself saying "I think about running too. I mean, when you look at how ineffective so many people in office seem to be, and when you see someone like Aaron Winters running, you think we should be able to do better."
Linda shook her head. "The problem is, your whole life is open to scrutiny. They tear apart every youthful indiscretion. Have you ever cut in line at the grocery store? Told an off color joke? Looked at somebody cross-eyed? It's ridiculous! Why would you

put yourself through that?"

"Politics have been dirty in this country since its founding," Ray said in rejoinder. "Have you read what Jefferson and Hamilton said about each other? Now *that* was nasty."

"Would you like an Aaron Winters button?" asked a pert young woman. We declined. "How about a bumper sticker?" No thank you to that also.

"Would you be interested in volunteering on his campaign?" asked another woman, thrusting a clipboard with a sign-up sheet in our direction. We declined again (politely I hoped).

"How about answering some questions?" asked an earnest young man, proffering a survey. That we did.

"I hope we really screwed up his statistics," Marcia said, turning away offers of coffee mugs, refrigerator magnets and who knows what else.

"I rest my case," Bob muttered, swatting at people offering campaign tokens. "This is ridiculous. And expensive." I thought mild mannered Bob was going to hit the person who offered him a cap with Aaron Winters' name emblazoned on its bill.

We finally made our way to six seats near the front of the auditorium. Patriotic music piped into the room. It was followed by the Pledge of Allegiance, an ecumenical invocation and opening words of praise for Aaron Winters. Then the candidate himself appeared, hair perfectly coiffed, whitened teeth gleaming, perfect family in tow.

"You'd think he was running for president, not town council," Bob snorted, slouching in his seat.

It did seem like overkill, I thought. But maybe people with big ambitions started out grandiose from day one.

We listened to Aaron Winters' canned speech. Actually, he had some good ideas. If I hadn't already decided to dislike him, he could have earned my vote.

Then it was time to meet the candidate. The six of us hung back, deflecting advances from campaign volunteers until the greeting line had dwindled. When we reached the end of the line, Ray took the lead. "You knew a friend of ours," he said, shaking Win-

ters' hand enthusiastically.
"Indeed? Who is that?" Winters responded avuncularly, missing Ray's use of past tense.
"Liz Williams," Ray replied, searching the candidate's face.
"Liz!" Winters exclaimed, releasing Ray's hand in mid-shake. "Her death is such a tragedy. To think something like this could happen in Summer Hill. Yes, poor Liz was very interested in helping with the campaign."
"Or was she more interested in derailing it?" Bob asked, surprising us all.
"That's preposterous," Winters sputtered.
"Is it?" Bernice asked. "We saw the two of you at dinner. Didn't look like campaign talk to us."
"What do you want?" the politician said, lowering his voice to a whisper.
"What Liz wanted," Bob replied. Where was this coming from? Our gentle, retiring accountant seemed to have transformed into a tiger.
"You go, honey," Marcia whispered.
Aware people were watching our exchange, Aaron Winters pasted a smile onto his face. "She bled me dry," he pleaded. "I can't pay any more."
"She blackmailed you and you killed her," Marcia said, her small hands balling into fists.
"What? Are you crazy?" Winters raised his voice, causing his wife's head to swivel in our direction. Linda wiggled her fingers at her and the woman waved back tentatively. "I think I'll go chat with Patty," she said.
"No," Winters said. "Please."
"If you killed Liz, you son of a bitch," Bob said, poking him in the chest, "I won't rest until you rot in Hell."
Winters blanched. "Are you crazy? That woman..."
"That woman. That woman." Bob was almost panting. "That woman was our friend. She was sick and we didn't know it. She had a f...king brain tumor. We might have been able to save her if we'd known. And you...you..."

Marcia, eyes huge, was pulling on Bob's arm. "Honey..."
Ray wrapped an iron strong arm around his friend's shoulders. "Come on, Buddy," he said, urging Bob to turn away. "We have to go."
"I didn't kill her," Winters whispered. "Please believe me, I didn't kill her."
I looked him up and down. "I hope you're telling the truth. In spite of what you might think, we don't want anything from you except for you to get what you deserve if you killed our friend. We're going to make sure the police take a good, hard look at you, Mr. Winters, if they haven't already. I'd guess they haven't looked very hard if you're going ahead with all this." I gestured toward the others. "We're done with you for now," I said, "but you should talk to your wife. I doubt we're the only ones who knew what you were up to."
The man looked as though he might faint.
"And don't count on our votes," Marcia said, "I'm voting for what's his name."
Together we turned heel and walked away.
We retreated to the pub in our neighborhood for food and drink and to rehash the evening's events. The pub was a beamed structure with a low roof and bottle glass windows. It sat in the middle of a beautiful garden overflowing with antique roses, lamb's ear, and other herbaceous plants. Outside tables were full of people in search of nibbles and alcohol, while the interior offered more sedate customers a tasty selection of burgers, barbecue, fish and chips and daily specials.
By the time we sat down, Bob had reverted to his normal persona. Marcia had visibly relaxed, no longer pulling on her green hair and crying out for the help of a saint whose name the rest of us had never heard before. We suspected she made her up on the spot.
Ray muscled his way to the bar. He brought back two foaming mugs of beer and slapped one on the table in front of Bob. He sat down and circled the second mug with his large hands.
"All righty, then," said Linda. "It's my turn." She took our drink

orders. After she came back, we sipped in silence.
A waitress approached our table. "I'll have the burger with bacon, cheddar cheese and barbecue sauce," said salad loving Bernice. "And fries on the side." 'All righty then' indeed.
"I'm sorry," Bob said. "I guess everything hit me all of a sudden."
"It's OK, Sweetie," Marcia said, sipping her beer and patting his knee. She looked bright eyed around the table. "Bob's actually quite passionate," she said. "He just hides it well. Why just the other night..."
"Marcia."
The one word seemed to shut her down. "You're right," she said. "Why am I trying to make light of things? Why do I do that?" Tears made their way down her cheeks.
"Now Sweetheart," Bob said, taking her hand, "Maybe I *am* passionate. But let's keep that our little secret, OK? Otherwise they'll never trust me to do their taxes again."
"At least we don't have to think about that for a while," Bernice said. "I don't know how you can do it every year."
The tension level at the table began to lower.
Ray ran his finger around the edge of his mug. "Aaron Winters may be a horse's patootie," he said, "but somehow I don't think he's our guy."
Linda sighed. "I don't know why, but I agree with you. Darn. It would have been such a nice solution. A scumbag goes to jail and our friends are off the hook."
Our appetizers arrived. We discussed Aaron Winters' proposals for revamping an underused public golf course. "I really like his ideas," Bernice said.
"I have a feeling he's going to pull out of the race." Marcia said. "It's not too late for you to throw your hat into the ring, Ray." She smiled teasingly.
Bernice narrowed her eyes at her husband. He looked into his beer. "You're serious, aren't you?" she asked.
Pandemonium broke out at the table. Bob was scribbling ideas on the back of a napkin. Linda was pounding keys on her phone. "You're a celebrity," Bob said excitedly. "We can play that up.

Being high school principal should be a plus too."
"Except that needs to stay non-political," Ray protested.
"I know we can raise money from some of our friends," Bernice said. We turned to stare at her. She smiled "What Ray wants, I want," she said. No wonder their marriage was so tight.
"I suspect if Patty finds out about the affair Aaron Winters will pull out of the race faster than you can say Jack Robinson," Linda said.
"Who was he anyway?" Marcia asked.
"Probably a fictional figure," Bob replied, "No one knows for sure. Some think it was in tribute to an officer of the court who had a man arrested, convicted and hanged in a matter of hours back in the 1700's."
We were impressed. The man was a fountain of knowledge in addition to being a good accountant.
"I hate to bring us back to today, but we need to make sure Riley Furman knows about Liz's affair with Winters and the fact that she was blackmailing him. It's not for us to decide whether he's guilty or not." I sipped my beer. "One of you needs to talk to Riley. I don't think we're speaking."
"After that kiss?" Marcia said, raising her eyebrows.
"What kiss?" Bob asked in confusion.
I expected Marcia to answer, but suddenly my friends were staring at me. "What's wrong?" I asked. "Do I have lipstick on my teeth?"
Linda cleared her throat and tilted her head to one side. I realized that my friend's eyes were focused just beyond my right shoulder. I turned. Riley Furman was standing behind me.
"Hello," he said.

CHAPTER TWENTY-TWO

He looked good. He looked really, really good, darn it.
He was dressed casually, clad in blue jeans that rode his hips and a form fitting grey tee shirt with an open blue and grey sports shirt over top. The man certainly had fashion sense. In one hand he held a long-neck beer bottle. His head was cocked slightly to one side and his dimples were on display. The colors of his shirts brought out the gray in his eyes, which crinkled at the corners showing off little laugh lines. My heart did a weird fluttering thing. I tried to ignore it.
"Detective!" Ray greeted him heartily, a bit too heartily in my opinion. "Join us?"
What was he doing? No, no, no, bad idea.
"Thanks, don't mind if I do."
A lot of shuffling and moving of chairs ensued, at the end of which I found myself sitting next to Riley. How in the world did that happen? I'd been trying to move in the opposite direction. I glanced around the table. Marcia was grinning. When she caught me staring at her she widened her eyes innocently. Next to her Linda was smiling behind her raised beer mug. What were my friends up to? My heart lurched. Were they trying to set me up with the detective? Even Bob had a self-satisfied smirk on his face. Oh no, this was not good. I tried to inch my chair away from Riley, but only succeeded in planting one of the legs on Riley's toe. He just smiled.
Our entrees arrived. I noticed that Riley had nothing placed in front of him. "Would you like to share my burger?" I asked. "Usually I take half home to Maggie, but she doesn't need it. She's spoiled enough as it is."
"Don't mind if I do," Riley replied.

I cut the burger in half.
"May I?" He snagged a French fry off my plate.
"Help yourself." I piled a handful onto an empty appetizer plate.
Conversation flowed surprisingly easily through the meal. Riley flagged down the waitress. "Could we have an order of puppy pops to go?" he said, referring to the dog friendly menu on the table.
"You don't have to do that," I protested.
"She's a cute little thing," he replied, "and I hate to deprive her of her burger. Although I understand onions are bad for dogs."
"I pick them off," I said a bit defensively.
"Do you have a dog?" Bernice inquired.
He shook his head. "I'd love to but my hours are too erratic. Hopefully I'll have one when that changes. I grew up with dogs and really miss having one."
"Do you ever work with the police dogs?" Linda asked.
"Only indirectly," he replied. "They are amazing animals. I remember one chasing a suspect up a tree. The guy was crying and begging us to take him. That dog sure had big teeth."
We laughed.
"I've worked with some of the search dogs, as well as the cadaver dogs," he said, his eyes clouding momentarily.
"I bet that could be tough," Bob said.
"It can," Riley agreed, "especially when you're too late to save someone." He noticed the serious looks on our faces. "Hey, but it's great when you find a lost kid. I swear the dogs are more excited than we are. You've never seen so much licking." We relaxed and laughed.
He sat back in his chair and eyed the rest of us. "So, what have you been doing tonight?"
We looked at each other in alarm. No one volunteered a response for a moment.
"We're just having dinner," Ray finally replied.
"Is that all?" Riley asked.
I wondered if we looked guilty.
"I'm asking because I got an interesting phone call this evening."

Riley said. "Aaron Winters claimed he was harassed by a bunch of crazy people who accused him of murdering Liz Williams. He said they accosted him at a political rally he was holding. He told me he was pretty embarrassed. Felt kind of threatened, too."

Winters would have been more embarrassed had his wife heard the conversation. And we threatened him all right. We intended to sic Riley Furman on him. And here he was.

"Why would you get the call?" Ray asked.

"The desk officer knows I'm working the case. She forwarded it to me."

"So it wasn't a coincidence your joined us here!" I exclaimed. "How did you find us?"

"I called your home."

"You did what?"

"Yep. I spoke to your son. He told me where to find you."

Nick was a traitor.

"He also said to ask you to bring home an order of Irish nachos."

As if.

A band had begun tuning up in the corner.

The detective leaned forward and looked each of us squarely in the eye. "What were you thinking, people? Did you expect Aaron Winters to hold out his hands for the cuffs and beg you to turn him over to us?" He snorted. "For your information we know something was going on between him and Liz Williams. You're not the only people in this town with eyes! Remember this is a small town and he's a well known man. People see things. They tell us. We've checked him out. We know the timeframe during which Mrs. Williams died. He has an alibi."

"Maybe he's lying," Marcia said.

"Do you think that didn't occur to us? It's rock solid. The mayor and the county attorney wouldn't cover for him."

We sat in glum silence.

"I don't know whether to be insulted by your sleuthing, lock you up for obstructing justice," (there he went again) "or chalk your behavior up to misplaced loyalty and maybe a touch of full moon lunacy." He sighed and raised an eyebrow. "How many times do

I have to tell you to stop? Please. I'm begging you." He looked appealingly at Ray. "You're an important figure in this community. He included Beatrice in his glance. "So are you. Do you want to get a reputation for being at best eccentric or at worst a meddling busybody?"

Ray looked thoughtful. Bernice crossed her arms over her chest, never a good sign. "I'm not letting my friend go to jail for something he didn't do."

"What if he did it?" the detective said.

Bernice continued to look stubborn. "I can't believe that someone who's been a friend for over twenty years is a murderer."

Bob challenged Riley. "Can you prove Dan killed Liz?"

"I'm sure you know I can't reveal anything connected with an on-going investigation. Right now, I'm not saying Dan killed his wife. I'm not saying he didn't either."

What the heck did that mean?

"Think back on what you know so far," Riley suggested. "And I do mean what you know, not what you think or what you feel. You'd have to agree that there are some holes in Dan's story."

"There are holes in Lexie's story also," Linda said.

"I agree. There's a good possibility they can be filled. Her father's holes are more gaping."

"I still can't believe it," Bernice protested, shaking her head.

"Remember that killing someone is not automatically the same as murder. Murder is an intentional act. You can kill someone in a fit of rage, or out of fear, and not be a murderer. Maybe that will make you think differently."

We digested that piece of information.

Riley held his hands out toward Bernice. "Please, please think about what I'm saying. Believe me when I tell you I know what I'm doing."

"People make mistakes, even the police," Bernice responded.

"Of course they do," Riley said, "And I'm not infallible. Give me a chance. And at least be careful. We don't need a repeat of the attack on Jackie."

Bernice nodded reluctantly.

The detective sighed again. "Clearly you've been holding down the liquor consumption for my benefit. Let me stand you one more round." He signaled the waitress, placed the order including another beer for him, stood up and held his hand out in my direction. "Would you dance with me?"

I looked around wildly. "What? Who? Oh, me? No, I don't think so...I..."

The dimples reappeared. "Come on, Jackie. I'm off duty. I don't bite. Dance with me."

Somehow I seemed to have risen from my chair. He took me by the hand and led me to the dance floor. Marcia had that goofy grin on her face again. If I had been able to reach her I would have strangled her. Just as well I was heading in the opposite direction.

We danced a lot that evening. In fact, everyone at the table danced, the men taking turns dancing with Linda and me. Riley was a good dancer, a firm leader and light on his feet at the same time. I only stepped on his toes once. Well, maybe it was two or three times, but who was counting? The feel of his arms around me was pleasant, almost too comfortable. I wasn't sure I wanted to let my guard down around this man. In spite of that I felt myself relaxing.

We talked a lot that evening also, about everything but Liz's death. Riley spun some yarns about his detective experiences. We listened wide eyed. Then Ray started on football stories. The detective was an appreciative audience.

"There was this one tax return I worked on..." Bob started. We all just stared at him. "Just joking." Bob laughed. He had switched to drinking soda, declaring himself to be our designated driver. None of us had over-consumed in any event, but we were happy not to be getting behind the wheel. Riley was drinking water, having capped his alcohol consumption early on.

Ray glanced at his watch. "Hey, we need to get going. I have a bunch of stuff to do tomorrow."

We said our farewells to Riley. He gazed a little longer than usual into my eyes but he didn't kiss me. I was surprised to feel a twinge of disappointment. As we walked to our cars I looked around at the group. Riley Furman seemed to fit in perfectly, as though he belonged with us. My heart did another flip flop. This might be the start of something good.

The detective drove away without a backward glance. Maybe I was wrong.

CHAPTER TWENTY-THREE

Once again Bernice, Linda, Marcia and I were sitting around my kitchen table. Bernice had brought over some of her famous carrot cake muffins and we were munching and sipping coffee, trying to plan our strategy.

"Riley Furman sure is a good dancer," Linda said.

"Mmhmm," I said, not really paying attention.

"The two of you looked good on the dance floor," Marcia said, reaching for the butter.

I frowned.

"Jackie," Bernice said. Something in her tone made me look up. "Honey, you know we love you, right?"

I nodded.

"It's been two years since Lars passed," she said gently.

I teared up. "I know that," I whispered.

"The point is," Marcia said in a tone that was solemn for her, "You didn't die with him."

My head jerked up and I opened my mouth to speak. I surveyed my friends' faces, full of love and compassion, and closed my mouth.

"We're not saying you have to fall in love, or have sex or do anything serious," Linda said, "but isn't it time you let yourself have some fun with a man who isn't Lars?"

I looked around the table. Obviously, these were things my friends had been wanting to say for a while now. I decided to let them have the floor.

"You know," Bernice continued. "Nick has been talking with Ray and me. He's worried about you."

"He is?" That came as a surprise.

She nodded. "He's thinking seriously of going to college nearby because he's concerned about what will happen to you if he leaves."

"But Nick has his heart set on going to Cal Tech," I protested. "He has for years."

"I know," Bernice said.

I thought a moment. Oh, crap. My son could talk to my friends but he couldn't talk to me? I studied Marcia and Linda's faces. "He talked to you too?" I asked weakly. They nodded. Double crap. What kind of mother was I that my son couldn't confide in me?

"He loves you," Linda contributed. "He doesn't want you to worry."

"So he worries instead?" I asked.

"It's OK," Marcia said, reaching out to hold my hand. "You and Nick have all of us. We're family."

Here came the tears again.

"We're just suggesting," Bernice said, "That you have some fun. Go on a date. Hold hands. Have dinner. It doesn't mean you're committing to anything."

"You think I should date Riley Furman, don't you?" I asked.

They nodded.

"Well, there's a slight problem in that he hasn't asked me out."

"He will," Linda the Oracle predicted. "When this mess with Dan and Lexie is over."

"Why does it have to be him?" I wailed. "Why can't it be someone else?"

"Knock yourself out," Marcia said. "We don't care who you go out with. We just want you to give it a try."

"How about Aaron Winters?" I asked. "He seems to be available."

We all laughed.

Marcia made herself another cup of coffee. "Now that's out of the way, are we any closer to figuring out who killed Liz?"

"I keep coming back to what Riley said last night," Bernice said. "Maybe it was Dan. Maybe he didn't mean to kill her."

"I'll tell you what," I said, pulling out a pad of paper and pencil, "Let's write down everything we know. And I mean know, don't suppose." I pushed the paper in Linda's direction. "Here. You have the best handwriting of any of us."

She nodded and picked up the pen. "Fire away."

"Liz had a brain tumor," Marcia contributed.

"Dan and Liz were fighting about money," Bernice said.

"Lexie thought her mother was trying to keep her away from her father,"

"Liz and Adam Wright were selling steroid prescriptions to college students," Linda said, scribbling as fast as she could.

"Liz was blackmailing women who had sexual relations with Adam Wright," Bernice said.

"Annalise Weiss and Dan Williams are in a relationship," Marcia said, moving her eyebrows up and down. Why was she doing that?

"Annalise went to confront Liz on Memorial Day after the party but she didn't go in," Linda said.

"Correction." I held up a finger. "She *says* she didn't go in."

"Good point," Linda said, nodding. "Focus on what we know, not what we've been told."

"Annalise claims she saw Dan's car parked outside Liz's house the night in question but Dan says he wasn't there." Marcia said.

"Lexie went to the fireworks but she didn't stay with her friends," I said.

"Dan was at a party at his sister's house. He claims he tried to find Lexie at the fireworks, but no one saw him there," Bernice said thoughtfully.

"Dan stayed with his parents that weekend," Linda said. "By the way, my hand is starting to hurt."

"We have to keep going," Marcia said. "I'll take over."

Linda shook her head "No way. Your handwriting is worse than the worst doctor's writing I've seen. And that's saying a lot. Onward." She shook her wrist. Fortunately, she wasn't using my fountain pen.

"Liz was having an affair with Aaron Winter and blackmailing him over it," Bernice contributed.

"Liz kept careful notes of her appointments," Linda said, frowning.

"Liz had an appointment with someone with the initials AW on Memorial Day," I said.

"Liz was stabbed," Bernice's voice was soft.

"There was an overturned table with a bottle of wine and two glasses next to Liz's body." Marcia scrunched her face thoughtfully and took a sip of coffee.

"Anything else?" Linda asked. She shook her wrist again. "We have sixteen things we know to be true."

"Read them slowly out loud," Bernice directed.

She did and we listened carefully.

"That bottle of wine and the glasses keep haunting me," I said. "It implies that this was a social meeting with someone who didn't scare or intimidate Liz."

"I think that's right," Marcia said. "That keeps bothering me too."

"Are we any closer?" Bernice asked. "Because if we're not, I think we need to leave it to the pros."

"Could I look at the list?" I asked. Linda pushed it toward me. I massaged my temples and studied it. "Could I see the calendar pages again?" More temple massaging. My friends drank coffee and stared at their own lists.

Finally I leaned back. "I have a theory," I told them, "But you're not going to like it."

"Spill," Marcia replied.

I did.

Bernice leaned forward and placed her head in her hands. I couldn't remember ever seeing her so dejected. "I don't like it," she said, "I don't want to believe it."

Linda and Marcia were frowning but beginning to nod.

"So how do we prove it?" Linda asked.

"We need to get back into Liz's house," I said, "and I think I'm in the best position to do it."

"Oh, no," Marcia protested, slamming her small fist on the table. "There is no way you're walking into danger by yourself. That is not happening."

By now Bernice and Linda's heads were bobbing up and down.

I held up my hand. "I appreciate what you're saying, but this is best done by one person and, being the next-door neighbor and closest of all of us to Lexie, it needs to be me. I'll be fine."

"Famous last words," Linda muttered.

"Let me call Lexie," I said. "I just need to ask her a couple of questions." I did and got the answers I expected.

"Are you going to share with us?" Bernice asked.

"I think there was something special about that Memorial Day appointment," I said. "And I think I know how to find out what it was."

"Does that mean your theory's right?" Linda asked.

I nodded slowly. "I'm afraid so."

Marcia sighed. "What a mess. What an awful mess." She raised her head and looked me in the eye. "But we're with you. Back to Liz's you go."

CHAPTER TWENTY-FOUR

The next morning dawned clear and bright. The temperature was already in the mid-seventies, promising a typically hot and humid June day in southeastern Virginia. I had promised to help Dan and Lexie sort through Liz's belongings, deciding which should go to charity and which were good candidates for the upscale consignment store downtown. I sighed as I rocked on the porch, sipping my second cup of morning coffee. In truth I had two motives for offering to help. Obviously, one was to assist my friends. The other was to grab one more opportunity to get inside that house and look around, hoping to find something that would prove that I was right as to the identity of Liz's killer. I sighed again. A cloudy or even rainy day would have seemed much more appropriate for the task at hand.

As I sighed and rocked, Dan pulled a small rented van into the driveway. Lexie followed in his car, clearly concentrating on her driving and trying to ignore comments from her grandmother, who sat ramrod straight beside her. I wondered what it might be like trying to operate a car as a team. Of course, Nick had accused me more than once of trying to drive from the passenger seat, so who was I to judge?

Dan gave me a wave and Lexie attempted a smile as she climbed out of the car. Her attempt didn't reach her eyes, and she looked pale and tired, her shoulders slumping and her motions slower than usual. Adele stepped out briskly, grabbing a box of empty garbage bags and heading toward the house. With one final sigh – I needed to stop doing that – it would just further depress the family – I put my coffee cup down on a side table and walked over to join Dan and Lexie in the driveway. After exchanging hugs I started lugging cardboard boxes inside the house.

"Why don't you work on Liz's clothes?" Dan suggested. "You have a good idea of what they're worth. I'm sure you'll know what to send to consignment and what to send to charity."

"Any suits Mom had are going to Dress for Success," Lexie informed me. "You should keep those separate."

"Understood."

"I can do this," Adele protested. "Jackie really doesn't need to help."

"I think Mrs. O should do it," Lexie said. "She was Mom's friend. She'll be careful with her stuff." Tears started to fall. "You might not. You didn't like Mom. You don't care what happens to her things."

Grandmother and father both looked shocked, as was I.

"Lexie..." Dan started.

"Lexie, that's not true," her grandmother managed to say.

"You liked her until she got sick," Lexie said. "Then you didn't like her anymore."

Boy, was this awkward. I wished I could think of an excuse that would allow me to escape, but Lexie's pleading eyes were on me and I was on a mission. Justice for Liz, I told myself, justice for Liz.

"We have tissue to use in folding the consignment clothes," Adele informed me, handing me a big stack of the stuff. She practically threw it at me. Oof! "Thanks," I said. What in the world did that woman have against me?

"You can have anything of Liz's that you'd like," Dan said. "And if there's anything you think one of the other ladies would want, feel free to set it aside."

"Thanks," I said again. As nice as Liz's things might be, I didn't think I'd use anything that would remind me of a murdered friend. But then again, who knew? I'd keep an open mind. Maybe something to remember the old Liz by would be nice.

"Except her jewelry," Adele said. "That stays with the family."

"Liz had a lot of nice costume jewelry," Dan said, glaring at his mother, "Jackie can have any of that she wants. You're going to inventory the real stuff, Mom. It's in the safe in the den." That sounded like marching orders to me. With a sniff Adele turned

and marched down the hall.
"Dad's going to sell the house when this is all over," Lexie said. "I'm going to look at Mom's figurines and stuff and decide what I want to keep."
"We might as well start staging the house now," Dan said. "Buyers seem to expect that these days."
In my opinion the house looked picture perfect as it was, but I supposed packing up some of the more personal decorations made sense. "I'm off then," I said, hefting the tissue paper and the box of garbage bags.
"I'll drop off some boxes in the bedroom," Dan said. He put a hand on my shoulder. "And, Jackie, thank you so much for doing this. I'm not sure Lexie and I could."
I nodded, blinking back tears, and headed toward the master bedroom. Once there I threw open the door to Liz's walk-in closet and simply stared at the array of clothes and accessories. I felt tears running down my cheeks and grabbed a tissue from a box on her nightstand. Maybe I could allow myself one more sigh. I reached into the closet and grabbed a large armful of clothes. I sat a pad and pen on the nightstand, preparing to document what was going where. Liz's wardrobe was impressive. Most of her clothes were in top notch condition and the list of consignment goods soon was longer than the list of things to be given to charity. I took things off hangers, wrote down estimated prices, folded garments in tissue paper and cried. After a while the tears stopped and I worked more efficiently. My mind started to concentrate not on the task at hand, but on where I might find evidence of a murderer's identity. I had an idea of one place to look but it was outside the bedroom and I hesitated to take a break from my task too soon. I lifted a group of pocketbooks off a shelf and tossed them onto the bed. A beautiful brown leather bag caught my eye. I held it to my nose, taking in the scent of the leather. I massaged the bag with my thumbs. It was soft and pliable, one of the most luxurious bags I'd ever held. Even so, it was practical and I knew I would use it. I hesitated, and then put it to one side. Maybe I would keep one memento. At least I

could consider it. I emptied all the bags of their contents. There was nothing of interest, just used lipsticks, a variety of pens, packages of tissues and other worthless objects. I snapped open a garbage bag and started to throw the contents inside. As I did so, I thought I heard a noise outside the bedroom windows. One side of the room boasted windows that ran almost from floor to ceiling, letting tremendous amounts of sunshine into the room. They slid open to allow fresh breezes during months when we didn't need air conditioning or heat in Virginia. Behind them was a row of hedges, interspersed with flowers on the outside of the border. I stopped and listened. There the noise was again. I tiptoed to the window and looked out. I couldn't see anything but I was sure something or someone was there. I thrust the window to one side and leaned out. "What the heck?"

Marcia was crouched in the shrubbery. She stood sheepishly, brushing leaves out of her hair and off her pant legs. "What in the world are you doing here?" I asked.

"Protecting you,' she replied. "Like a bodyguard."

I shook my head. "You must be kidding."

"No, I'm not." She put her hands on her hips. "You wouldn't let us come with you and we have no idea what you might find. I'm not letting you go into danger alone."

I didn't know if I should hug her or strangle her. "I'm fine," I insisted.

"You may be fine now, but we don't know what might happen. I'm staying here."

"Oh, for Pete's sake."

"Someone's coming!" Marcia dipped below the window sill and I slid the window shut.

"Is everything all right?" Dan asked, eying me from the doorway.

"Yes, absolutely," I said, wheeling around. "I was just taking a break and admiring the landscaping. You guys did such a nice job with it."

"Thanks," he replied, still looking a bit uncertain. He glanced around the room. "Looks like you've made a lot of progress. Are some of these boxes ready to go?"

I nodded. He lifted two of the boxes and carried them toward the waiting van. Marcia's head popped up again. "Go away!" I hissed. "You're going to get caught."

"Am not!"

I threw up my hands and turned back to my task, deciding to ignore my protector. I decided to attack Liz's lingerie drawers for a while, knowing that her intimate apparel would have to be thrown away. I pulled out a handful of underwear and admired its amazing silkiness. Never in my life had I splurged on truly expensive undergarments. Lars had teased me about my sensible bras and panties, but they hadn't deterred his enthusiasm for late night encounters. Occasionally he had gifted me with a pretty nightgown. I had kept those for vacations and other romantic occasions and let him happily remove my sensible nightshirts and pajamas other times.

I reached further into the drawer. My fingers encountered something that felt like a checkbook. I pulled out a calendar, the kind you used to get for free in card stores. I rifled through it. The notations were for the current year. I flipped to the entries for Memorial Day. There is was. "AW". I took a deep breath and slipped the calendar into the brown pocketbook I had been coveting. I glanced at my watch, wondering if it was too soon to pause in my efforts. I had been working for over an hour. Nothing like the present.

I left the bedroom and headed for a kitchen. If anyone stopped me I would tell them I was going to get a glass of water. The house was quiet, each family member apparently working on his or her own.

I entered the kitchen and stood in front of the refrigerator. A colorful calendar was attached to it with magnets. The prior evening Lexie had told me that Liz listed only family events on that particular calendar. I lifted the page to reveal the Memorial Day square. "AW". I closed my eyes and took a shaky breath. Bile rose in my throat.

"What are you doing?"

I spun around. Adele Williams' dark eyes were darting between me and the calendar. "I came in for a glass of water."

"Then where's your glass? And what are you doing snooping in Liz's calendar?" she asked, stepping toward me.

I tried to move away but found myself jammed against the refrigerator.

"Give that to me!" Adele commanded, reaching out her hand.

"Give you what?" I asked, my eyes seeking an escape route.

"The calendar!" she hissed. "Stop playing games with me."

"Don't you think someone will miss it?" I suggested. "Liz always kept a calendar here."

"Give it to me," Adele insisted. To my horror she reached behind her. Her fingers curled around the handle of a knife inserted into a block standing on the counter behind her.

"You killed her!" I said loudly, hoping I would be heard. "You killed Liz! Why would you do that?"

Adele advanced further. "You stupid woman! Give me that calendar."

I shook my head.

"All your meddling," Adele ranted, "poking your nose in where it wasn't wanted. You've ruined everything." She gestured with the knife. "Liz was ruining my family. She was hurting Lexie and what she was doing to Dan..." She took a step closer and I did a sort of sideways crab crawl, feeling my way along the refrigerator toward the open space of the patio.

"Liz was sick," I said.

"Well, I couldn't know that, could I?"

"How are you going to get away with killing me" I asked, stalling for time.

Adele looked puzzled. Clearly she hadn't worked that out. "I'll tell them you attacked me," she said triumphantly. "Yes, that will do it. You killed Liz because you wanted Dan for yourself and when I figured it out you tried to kill me." The lady was definitely loony tunes.

Desperately I wondered if Marcia had followed me toward the pool area next to the kitchen. Even if she hadn't Lexie and Dan couldn't be far away. I opened my mouth to scream.

"Mom?" Dan stood in the entrance to the kitchen.

Bernice and Linda burst through the door to the patio waving their cell phones, Marcia hot on their heels. "I called 911!" Bernice said.

"And I called Dan," Linda said. She turned to Adele, who was still holding the knife. "I had you on speaker. We heard every word you said."

"Mom?" Dan repeated, holding onto the kitchen island with white knuckles. Behind him Lexie had run up and was staring at the scene wide eyed.

"Grandma?"

Adele whirled to face her son and granddaughter.

"Mom, what did you do?" Dan asked, hesitantly moving toward her, holding his hands out in front of him.

"I didn't mean to," Adele pleaded. She dropped the knife she was holding and stumbled toward her son with her arms outstretched. "I came to talk to her. I thought I could make her see reason, see what she was doing to you. I wanted to convince her to let Lexie live with you or us." She turned toward her granddaughter. "What she was doing with Lexie was shameful. Turning her away from you, parading all her so-called dates in front of her, making her go out with those college boys…" She nodded. "Oh yes, I knew all about it. Lexie told me some things. I heard others around town. And what she was doing to you, Dan…" She continued moving toward her son, who stood as though paralyzed. "She laughed at me. She said some terrible things. I got so angry I grabbed the knife from the barbecue. She laughed at me and I…I stabbed her." She sagged against the kitchen counter.

Lexie's face was a study in shock. Bernice moved around the island and threw her arms around the girl.

Dan seemed to stumble but in reality someone had pushed him aside. Riley Furman stood where Dan had been a second before, his hand resting on the handle of his gun, his gray eyes trained on Adele Williams. "Mrs. Williams?" he said softly.

Adele dropped her head into her hands. "I did it for you, son," she said. "I did it for you and Lexie."

Riley slid his eyes toward me. I was still standing next to the refrigerator, bookended by Linda and Marcia. "Fortunately, I was in the area when we got the call," he said. He shook his head. "Miss Marple, what am I going to do with you?"

"I don't know, but these last minute rescues have to stop, Inspector Barnaby," I said.

He smiled.

CHAPTER TWENTY-FIVE

A light breeze was stirring the wind chimes on Marcia's porch. She, Bob, Bernice, Ray, Nick, Max, the dogs and I sat on mine, sipping iced tea and eating ham biscuits. Idea! Put the recipe in my book. Hey, this could be fun after all.

Dan and Lexie pulled into the driveway next door. They were followed by a woman in an SUV bearing a real estate logo. Lexie and her father approached us.

"We're moving away," Lexie said softly. We looked inquisitively at Dan. "Far away." Lexie said.

"My boss has been fantastically supportive," he said. "She managed to get me transferred to our office in Orlando. Lexie and I talked it over. We agreed we need a new start."

"What about the promotion?" Ray asked.

Dan's face broke into the first genuine smile we'd seen in a long time. "It came through. I'll be able to work from home most of the time now. Florida's as good a place as any to live."

"What about…you know?" Marcia was sending semaphores with her eyebrows.

"You mean Annalise?" Lexie asked.

We were all taken aback.

"I've met her," Lexie said. "She's all right."

"We're taking that slow," Dan said. "She may come down to visit in a couple months, but we'll see how Lexie feels about it then. Annalise agreed there's no hurry."

I was happy that some of what we said to her when we were at the conference seemed to have sunk in.

Lexie gave a mischievous grin and stuck an elbow in her father's ribs. "After all, I'll be going to college in a couple years. I'd hate for Dad to get too lonely."

Dan gave his daughter a quick hug.
"Dad says I can apply for a summer job at Disney World next year," Lexie almost looked excited.
"Hey, that would be cool," Nick said. "Maybe I could come down and work there too." He glanced at me. "Or maybe not."
I laughed.
"Think about next year," Dan said. "You could stay with us." He swiveled his head. "You too, Max. And Bill if he wants to."
"How could you possibly have room for all of them?" Marcia asked.
"We've found a good sized house. There will be plenty of space."
Nick looked at me hopefully. "Don't jump the gun," I warned him. "A year is a long time away." He still looked hopeful, probably noting that I hadn't said 'no'. Yet. Well, we'd see.
"Before you go, do you want to shoot some hoops?" Nick asked Lexie. She looked at her father, who nodded his assent.
"Can I..."
I raised my eyebrows.
"May I use the car?" my son asked.
"You know where the keys are." I smiled. I noticed Lexie slip her hand into Nick's as they walked to the car. I wondered if that relationship would go anywhere. It was unlikely, but she was a very nice girl. Max trailed behind them, calling Bill, who was across the street, to join them. For a moment I wondered about Nick's brilliant Asian girlfriend, whom I still hadn't met. Oh well, at this point it was none of my business. On the other hand, part of me was glad the boys were going along to chaperone Nick and Lexie, not that they were aware that was what they were doing. On the other hand...oh, never mind. I took a sip of tea.
Dan approached the railing. "Jackie," he said, "I'm so sorry. When I think of what my mother could have done to you..."
"Did you suspect she killed Liz?" I asked.
Dan shook his head. "Never in a million years. I knew she was upset with Liz, but she's my mother. Of course she would be." He put his hand on the rail. "She's not a bad person."
No, she wasn't, I reflected. I still didn't like her, but that was

neither here nor there. I was a mother too. Who knows what I would do to protect my son? I glanced at Bernice and Marcia. Who knows what any of us would do to protect our children? Even Linda's protective instinct for her nieces was very strong. I covered Dan's hand with mine.

"What happens now?" Ray asked.

"We'll see. She's been charged with second degree homicide. If that sticks, I don't know what the system will do to her, given her age. I can't imagine her going to jail. Her attorney thinks he can bargain the charges down to manslaughter, maybe even involuntary manslaughter. In that case he thinks she might just get probation. He seems to be pretty good."

"Who is it?" Linda asked.

"Aaron Winters."

Bob choked on his biscuit and Marcia pounded him soundly on the back.

"What about your father?" I asked. "What is he going to do?" I felt sorry for the elderly man, who had always seemed so pleasant. Lexie had told Nick that his wife's arrest had sent him into such deep shock and depression that his doctor had admitted him to the hospital.

"Dad's sticking by Mom. We offered him the chance to come with us, but he's staying here. In spite of everything, he still loves her." Oh, the course of true love. Talk about for better or worse. I admired the gentleman. If only more of us would take our marriage vows as seriously.

The real estate agent had been walking around the property making notes and was now standing on the porch of Dan's house, patiently waiting. "I'd better go," he said. "We have a lot of things to decide before we list the house."

"We'll keep an eye on things if you're not here," Ray promised.

All of us ladies hugged Dan. The men did that back thumping, almost hugging thing men do. We parted with mutual promises to stay in touch. Somehow, unless that was done through our children, I suspected we would soon lose contact.

Dan left. The rest of us settled back in, eating, drinking, and talking about recent events. Shortly after we refreshed our glasses of tea we heard the distinctive 'thump bump, thump bump' of a Harley Davidson motorcycle. "That thing sounds like it would shake you to death," Bernice commented.

"Nice bike," Ray said appreciatively as it turned onto our street, chrome gleaming in the sun. "I have to get me one of those."

Bernice gave him her patented glare. Then she smiled. "If you get one, I get one too."

"It's a deal!" Ray said. He pointed at all of us. "You're my witnesses. You heard it here."

The rider pulled to a stop and dismounted in front of my house. When he pulled off his helmet, we recognized Riley Ferguson, decked out in riding gear including leather chaps.

"Hey, Riley!" Ray called. "Come up and have some tea."

The detective ducked his head almost shyly. "Actually," he said, "I've come to ask Jackie if she'd like to go for a ride." He leaned down to pat Maggie, who was running ecstatic circles around him, jumping straight up and trying desperately to kiss his face. "Maybe we'll get a sidecar for you, pup," he said.

I surveyed the approving expressions on my friends' faces along with Riley's hopeful one. As I did, I had an epiphany. My next series would feature a group of smart, gorgeous mystery-solving women. Maybe I'd throw in a handsome detective as a bonus. And there would be no recipes. Not a one.

I smiled at Riley. "Why not? Sounds like fun."

ACKNOWLEDGEMENT

Many thanks to my wonderful book group friends,
Barbara, Marliese, Debbie, Mary Kay, Peggy, Marty and
Pat for reading and critiquing my first book. Your ideas made it better. I hope you'll put up with reading the others as they come along. Thanks also to my first readers, Jennie, Mary and Cathy, particularly to Mary the grammar guru!

ABOUT THE AUTHOR

Allie Ross

Allie Ross grew up reading mysteries, starting with Nancy Drew and the Hardy Boys and graduating to the classics by authors such as Agatha Christie and Dorothy Sayers. She put aside her dreams of writing for many years, practicing law for thirteen years and then working as a certified financial planner for twenty-five. With retirement came a chance to write. She now divides her time between North Carolina and Florida, living with her husband, Jim, and one very spoiled boxer. When not cooking, quilting or line dancing she is working on other books in this series.

Made in the USA
Middletown, DE
19 February 2024

49472664R00132